THE DEAD SHALL TEACH THE LIVING

A Mystery Novel

RM Kureekattil

ISBN: 1974606007
ISBN 13: 9781974606009
Library of Congress Control Number: 2017914903
CreateSpace Independent Publishing Platform
North Charleston, South Carolina

Front-cover credits: Tony Thuruthel, Jerome Thobjornsen and Amol Mathew.

For my wife, Valentina (Tinakutty)

CONTENTS

PROLOGUE: APRIL 20, 2001

Life is weaker than death, and death is weaker than love.

—Khalil Gibran

Raj stirred in his bed and opened his eyes. There was something stuck to his face. His mind was clouded, and he did not understand why his hands were restrained or why curtains surrounded him. There was a small television screen on the wall, which he did not remember seeing when he went to bed.

The young patient tried in vain to free his hand to pull the oxygen mask away from his face.

He screwed up his eyes and tried to focus on the floating white apparition in the room. The image slowly became sharper, taking the form of a young nurse, who had bent down and was adjusting his drip.

"You're lucky to be alive," he heard the nurse mutter matter-of-factly.

Raj could make out the nurse walking back to her desk where the resident was taking notes. She must have told the doctor something, for the resident got up from his chair and approached the patient, shining a torch into his eyes. With his thumb, he pressed hard on Raj's forehead. The pupillary reflex to light and response to pain were the early responses a doctor would seek in persons emerging from coma.

Raj grimaced in an attempt to scream, but before he could utter any sound, he drifted back into the blissful state of semiconsciousness.

Dr. Ian Lambert went back to his desk and wrote Raj's progress in his chart.

The young man remained in the intensive-care unit for one more day. His wife was allowed to visit him, and it was only then that he could put the pieces of the puzzle together.

Raj remembered being admitted to the hospital for severe abdominal pain and jaundice. He vaguely remembered being discharged.

"You can go home now," his doctor had said after his symptoms had abated. He had gone back to his unit that Friday afternoon and had telephoned his wife.

"I'm taking the flight to Perth from Adelaide tomorrow night," Vidya had told him. "From Perth, I'll catch the one o'clock red-eye flight and should reach Broome by four in the morning." She'd then added, "Don't come to the airport if you are not well."

The reunion with her husband had not happened the way she had hoped it would. Vidya sat beside Raj on his hospital bed. A teardrop meandered its way down her beautiful face, and she brushed his hair with her left hand. She looked tired. The young man smiled weakly at her.

"Tell me what happened," he said.

"Why did you do that?"

"Why did I do what?" Raj was surprised at Vidya's response.

Vidya was quiet for some time. Then she said quietly, "You know what happened."

"Maybe I don't. Tell me what happened."

"No, only when you get home." She turned away and stared out the window.

"I want to know now." Though his voice was low and his face drawn, the familiar firmness in his voice made her realise that he would continuously harass her till she told the story. Vidya relented.

"Well, I wanted to give you a surprise. I told you I was flying on Saturday night, but I had actually booked the flight for Friday night. I reached here on Saturday morning, around four thirty." She wiped her tears with a tissue.

"I reached the unit at about five. You didn't answer the door-bell." Vidya paused for a moment and looked intently at her husband, trying to fathom his thoughts.

Raj returned the gaze steadily. His wife continued. "I wondered if you had gone back to the hospital, so I tried ringing you. Then I heard your phone ringing in the unit. I walked around to the side and peeped through the window. The windowpane was broken. You were lying on your back on the bed with your mouth open, and there was blood oozing from your nose."

On seeing her husband in that state, Vidya had cried out hysterically and had run to the front of the unit. The nurse next door, who was coming back after her night shift, had called the ambulance and got Raj to the hospital.

"Please get me my folder," Raj said. Vidya got up slowly and returned with it. There was weariness in her walk that betrayed both tiredness and sorrow.

"Carbon-monoxide poisoning as a result of suicide attempt from car exhaust fumes," Raj read.

"Your car was parked next to your unit. There was a hose connecting the muffler of your car to the air-conditioning vent." Vidya looked at her husband intently, trying again to fathom his thoughts.

"Well, let me remember."

Raj paused for a while. He stared at the ceiling, trying to think. Vidya stared at him for a short while and then looked down at the floor dejectedly. With her right elbow resting on her thigh, she supported her chin with the palm of her hand. It was about five minutes later that her husband started talking. He spoke haltingly, pausing between each word to take the time to think.

"You said the window was broken?"

"Yes, there was a cricket ball inside the room."

"The kids must have broken the window that afternoon."

"What kids?"

"Urchins—they play cricket all the time. But the main reason that I am alive is..." Raj's voice trailed off.

"Is what?" she prompted.

"Is"—Raj paused—"your love."

With newfound energy, Raj pulled Vidya towards him, hugging her tightly in gratitude and starting to kiss her hungrily. There was the sound of a chair scratching on the floor as though somebody was getting up, and Vidya's Indian prudence did not allow this overt expression of love to continue. She freed herself from her husband's embrace and moved to the far side of the bed. She then turned slowly and looked at her husband with extreme sorrow.

"What made my husband, whom I love so dearly, do it?"

CHAPTER 1

THE FLIGHT TO BROOME—
NOVEMBER 30, 2000

Ela nakki nayude kiri nakki naya.
("Like the dog that would lick the lips of the dog that
had licked clean the thrown-away banana leaf.")

It was a rather unremarkable year for Raj's motherland, India. The country was ruled by the Hindu nationalist party, Bharatiya Janata Party. It had been two years since India had conducted its second atomic-bomb detonations. September 11 was one year away.

The cruel joke called communism had long since collapsed, except in a few forgotten places in the world like Cuba and Kerala, a tiny, overpopulated, and beautiful state in South India. In Kerala, Raj's birthplace, shrivelled relics of a bygone era, who called themselves communists, still held sway over the masses, thanks to the corruption and ineptitude of their opponents in state politics: the Indian National Congress.

Raj landed in Broome one windy day at the end of November. The flight from Adelaide was bumpy. The in-flight news had announced that they were expecting a cyclone in the next day or two. Cyclones were not uncommon in this part of the world. But cyclones were the furthest thing from his mind during this bumpy ride.

Raj was starting a new job as a registrar in histopathology in Broome. During the flight his mind journeyed to the past—the rigorous medical-school training he'd undertaken in India, his becoming a doctor, and his decision to move from being a treating doctor to a lab doctor or pathologist.

Raj was a dreamer. Becoming a doctor was his mother's wish, like every mother's wish in Kerala. After getting his MBBS degree, he found that he did not have time for himself because somebody was always ill and requiring his attention.

His distaste for the profession was sown and began to grow when he worked as a missionary doctor in North India. There, Raj worked in a small hospital in a village in wayward Bihar, one of the most lawless places in the world, where he took total care of his patients.

As part of his routine, he would sometimes make house calls. Raj would drive to the patient's house. If he found that it was a difficult case, he would take the patient to the hospital in his old Jeep and test the patient's blood and urine himself. If an operation were required, he would anaesthetise the patient and perform the surgery, which often was an appendectomy or an amputation. The patient would sometimes need blood. Since Raj's blood group was the universal donor group—O negative—Raj would more than often donate his own blood, for the villagers were either too scared or too unhealthy to donate blood. He also did the postsurgical care. And if the patient died, the villagers would insist that Raj do the funeral rites.

It was then that an idea took birth and sparked a new ray of interest in his profession. Raj's attention turned to the diagnostic side of medicine, an occupation where a bearded, scholarly person would peer down a microscope all day long at somebody's blood, skin, breast, or testis sample to interpret the cause of the affliction. So he resumed his career in medicine by learning pathology, one of the oldest branches of medicine. Many of his relatives thought he was turning into a lab technician. He did not mind as long as his neighbours did not bother him with their coughs, haemorrhoids, constipation, or impotence during his brief visits home. Being a pathologist indeed made his mother proud, for she was a lab technician and felt she must have had a role in his decision to become a pathologist. When he was growing up, his mother had often related to him the various tests carried out in the labs in the hospitals, for she took great pride in her work.

His mind wandered back to his own journey from his native village of Thottumughom in Kerala to Australia, one of the most progressive nations in the world. Raj had always wanted to earn a Western medical degree and then move to a Western democracy. Raj and his wife, Vidya, had both recently received their postgraduate qualifications, he in histopathology and she in biochemistry, both from one of India's most reputable institutions, the Christian Medical College in Vellore, South India. Raj was planning to go to the United Kingdom to start working as an observer in a pathology lab when Vidya got a scholarship to work on a biochemistry project in Adelaide. Raj thought that he should accompany his wife to Australia and try his luck in the lucky country rather than fly to the United Kingdom and live thousands of kilometres away from his wife.

He had left behind potholed roads; rickety, crowded buses; strikes that made life impossible almost every other day; potbellied policemen, who harassed the common man; nuns in white habits, who caned and abused their pupils; and politicians and civil servants, who respected only those rich enough to grease their palms. They had a six-month visa, but they had taken a one-way ticket to Adelaide, Raj always willing to try his luck and take a chance. A one-way flight was slightly cheaper than a return flight, and Raj was optimistic that one of them would be able to find a job that would allow both of them to stay on in Australia after Vidya's six-month scholarship was over.

Luckily, Raj found a sympathetic head of the department of histopathology at the Royal Adelaide Hospital, who gave him a supernumerary position at her lab. She then gave him a good reference when he applied for the job in Broome. Their gamble to stay on in Australia appeared to have paid off when Raj got the news that he had landed a paid trainee registrar's position in Broome.

The poverty, or lack of money, which had been their constant companion since coming to Australia, soon ended. Vidya's scholarship fetched them $10,000 in Australian dollars for the six-month period. They got around $1,400 every month, from which the young doctor couple had to pay rent and buy food. Since they had come on a one-way flight, they also had to save money for the return flight, for there was only hope, but no assurance, that he or Vidya would get a job to stay on after her six-month term was over.

In India, their pay was small compared with Western standards, but they were rich by Indian standards. Here in the land of the rich, they were poor, extremely poor, for the Australian Government and the labour unions did not care about these foreign professionals who laboured in the hospitals or labs, as they were here to study on research grants and not to vote. But still the young couple had survived. They bought dried chickpeas and lentils and soaked them overnight before they cooked them as they did in India. Rice was not expensive. Their food was low in animal protein and green vegetables that they indulged in only occasionally and in small quantities when these items were on sale at the supermarket.

Ela nakki nayude kiri nakki naya (Like the dog that would lick the lips of the dog that had licked clean the thrown-away banana leaf.). Raj remembered the proverb his mother used to tease him with when he and his siblings fought over food. It was a custom in their part of India to use banana leaves as dinner plates.

And now, after months of poverty, they were finally going to be reasonably paid. Maybe they could now afford fish and chips and the occasional Victoria Bitter.

CHAPTER 2

DR. STICH AND ROYAL KIMBERLEY HOSPITAL

Vaidyan vidhichadum rogi ischichathum pal`e.
("The patient longed to have milk and that
is exactly what the doctor prescribed.")

D uring the flight, Raj's mind was preoccupied with thoughts about his new job and his new boss. He had heard a lot about Dr. Stich.

While he was applying for the position, Raj had consulted his mentor, the Director of Pathology at Adelaide Hospital. She had encouraged him to apply for the job, but towards the end of the meeting, she had said, "You will be all right with Dr. Stich. He is a great pathologist but just slightly odd," she had explained, though not to Raj's satisfaction, when he had enquired.

"Slightly eccentric," "difficult to work with," "a bit quirky," "short tempered," "odd": these were the opinions the other pathologists in Adelaide held about Dr. Stich when Raj had asked around.

Though apprehensive, the young doctor had accepted the position in Broome, for this was his only chance of getting a foothold in Australia.

Dr. Stich was waiting for Raj at the airport. Being the only Indian on the flight, Raj was easy to spot. And there were not many people on the flight—at the most, sixty—mostly people returning after escaping to the South for the summer break.

"And for me, this place is yet to be called home, at least for a year." The realisation passed through Raj's mind like a fleeting thought.

Raj was a shade lighter than charcoal or boot polish. For an Indian, he was tall, almost six feet. He was not fat, but not thin either, as his constant fight against the flab made him somewhere in-between.

"Welcome to Broome," Dr. Stich boomed in a thick European accent.

The portly doctor had a look of approval in his aged blue eyes. Raj's businesslike appearance must have pleased him. Though his blue cotton trousers and khaki T-shirt were slightly worn, they were neat and ironed. The young man's jet-black hair was cut short and neatly parted; his hair was mildly wavy and would have curled if allowed to grow longer.

"Thank you very much," Raj replied, smiling at Dr. Stich. The young doctor's face betrayed slight anxiety, which he tried to mask by making an effort to look cheerful. His eyes were widely placed and were decorated by arched eyebrows, which would have made Cleopatra jealous. They sat above a medium, slightly flat nose.

As they walked to the car park, Raj noticed that the elderly pathologist was not in the best of health. He had a pronounced double chin, his skin was puffy under the eyes, and his cheeks were swollen, possibly due to consuming generous amounts of alcohol. A potbelly hung over his belt, like an overfilled gunny bag, below which thin legs stuck out like matchsticks from beneath blue drill shorts. Dr. Stich wore a white cotton half-sleeved shirt that strained in the middle trying to accommodate his girth.

As the older man ambled along, his blue shorts flapped rhythmically. They were very wide, letting air in, and, like tradesman's shorts, they covered only the upper half of his skinny thighs. Working boots and long brown socks, folded neatly beneath the knees, partly hid the knotted veins worming across his calves. Dr. Stich reminded Raj of the expression "lemon on matchstick," one of the many phrases that doctors used in their extensive figurative lexicon. It was how they described the features of Cushing's syndrome, a malfunction of the adrenal gland, the main feature of which was obesity.

The crimson sky attested to the fact that night was fast approaching. Dark clouds, their bellies sodden, filled the horizon and slowly rolled towards them. Like a thousand lions roaring in unison, distant thunder sounded forebodingly. Like ghosts with craggy faces, pale gloomy shadows of hungry gum trees followed the two men as they trudged silently to the car park. Their sinuous branches would suddenly stretch as if to pounce on them and then retract at the same speed as the men passed from one streetlight to the next.

A shadow clouded Raj's mind as he glanced sideways at his new boss.

Raj heaved his baggage into the luggage space of the old Jackaroo four-wheel drive and slid into the front passenger seat. The jalopy grudgingly croaked into life and sputtered out of the airport, turning south onto Broome Road on the way to the hospital. The roads appeared deserted, except for occasional tourists, who, bent under their heavy backpacks, thronged the small curio shops run by the descendants of Chinese pearl divers. The obese Buddha in one of those shops smiled benignly at them, and Raj winked back. The car stopped at a red light, and a mixed aroma of

Chinese, Japanese, and Timorese cuisine wafted towards Raj from a roadside café.

Dr. Stich gazed gloomily at the road while he drove. His voice was even toned, and he sounded worn out from the travails of life. Creases marked his forehead, proclaiming that he was into his sixties and suggesting the years that had passed had not all been filled with mirth and laughter. Dr. Stich's long European nose was slightly hooked at the end, which made him look like a tired vulture.

"You know, I was the Director of Pathology at Queen Victoria Hospital in London," he announced.

"Were you?"

"I wrote the chapter on the liver in the Cambridge Textbook of Pathology."

"I've read that. It's very beautifully written."

"I was also Chairman of the Dermatopathology Association of the UK," he continued. His face had the solemn expression of a wise old Indian guru, who could levitate himself with meditation.

Raj looked at him in amazement. He thanked his stars and foresightedness in applying for the job.

"I'm happy that I came here," he said, a comment that appeared well received, as Dr. Stich's solemn mood momentarily gave way to a wide grin.

On their way to the hospital, Raj learnt that Dr. Stich was a master of all that was known in pathology. It seems he had discovered most things, or he was an authority in most of the sub-specialties in pathology. Skin, endocrinology, infectious diseases, the liver—the list grew longer and ended only when they reached Royal Kimberley Hospital. Raj later learnt that Dr. Stich cut his own hair, pulled out his own teeth with a pair of pliers, and cut off his small skin cancers with a pair of scissors. He was even known to remove the batteries of his clocks before he went to bed every night to prolong their lives, though his actions defied logic and defeated the purpose of having the clock.

The air was thick and humid. The monsoon had delayed its arrival and had not yet cooled the top end of down under. Raj's boss dropped him off at his unit. His T-shirt clung to his damp body, and he pulled at its bottom to try to free it. There was a Telstra phone booth just opposite his unit. Raj fumbled in his pocket for his wallet and shook forty cents into his palm. He had told his wife that he would call her as soon as he reached Broome but had not yet done so, as he had been too preoccupied talking with the old pathologist.

"I'm fine," he told her. "It's hot and sticky, like Kerala. I'm sure you would like it here. Dr. Stich is not the person we thought he was. He is very nice."

"Is that so? Maybe your wishes will come true," she said, referring to Raj's desire to gain a Western medical degree. Vidya appeared happy with his news.

"*Vaidyan vidhichadum rogi ischichathum pal`e,*" he said.

"What's that?"

Though they both hailed from Kerala in South India, Vidya, having been brought up in North India, was not conversant with the intricacies of the Malayalam language.

"What's what?"

"What you just said."

"Well, the doctor prescribed milk, and that was exactly what you desired to have," Raj explained metaphorically. "Just as you wanted to come to a warm place, I got this appointment, and here I am in Broome—just as you wished." Raj paused.

"Just as you wished" was the response from the other side. "Get some rest. I'll talk to you soon."

"Talk to you soon." There was a click at the other end.

Raj hung up and looked around. Royal Kimberley Hospital was a three-storey building in the middle of a large car park. A small hill stood a few hundred metres from the hospital, shielding it from the setting sun. A thick fluffy cloud hung over the hill like a mop of curly hair, and from afar, the mountain resembled an indigenous elder standing in the middle of the Australian desert. Raj decided to call him Mr. Benjora Cobar. The young Indian doctor wondered what Mr. Cobar would have witnessed over the past eons. He may not have witnessed the separation of the Australian landmass from the super continent Gondwanaland, but he would certainly have seen the indigenous people arrive from across the Timor Sea around fifty thousand years ago and, of course, the early European settlers less than three hundred years ago. He must have beamed with pride when the indigenous kids wallowed in the mud around him, and he would have watched how they domesticated the dingo that arrived with Malayan sailors around four thousand years ago.

Mr. Cobar must have cried incessantly when the white settlers came with their guns, diseases, and new ways, subjugating a continent and scattering its people. He would have watched in dismay and sympathy when the Chinese were brought to dive deep into the seas for the beautiful pearls Broome is famous for. And more recently, Benjora would have sighed with relief when the indigenous people and the Chinese were given citizenship and voting rights.

Raj looked up at Mr. Cobar seeking benediction, but the revered elder appeared to be sad and smiled sympathetically at Raj, for Mr. Cobar seemed to know the dark future awaiting the dusky young Indian doctor.

CHAPTER 3

HIRANYAKASIPU

namas te narasimhaya
prahladahlada-dayine
hiranyakashipor vakshaha
shila-tanka-nakhalaye
("I offer my respectful obeisance unto You, Lord
Nrisimhadeva. You are the giver of pleasure to
Prahlada Maharaja, and your nails cut the chest
of Hiranyakashipu like a chisel cutting stone.")

R aj was put up in a detached two-room unit on the hospital campus. Though it looked like a shack, the unit was very comfortable. There was a bedroom, with an open-plan, combined living, dining, and kitchen en suite. It was air-conditioned, and he did not have to pay for power. Raj's unit was one of several, perhaps twenty in total, accommodating young doctors, nurses, lab technicians, and the occasional physiotherapist.

The morning after his arrival, Raj got up early and walked to the pathology lab, barely two hundred metres away. It was a brick-laid path and wound around tropical bushes and ornamental palms.

On his way to the lab, Raj found himself staring at a large ancient gum tree, which stood about fifty metres from the path. There was something strange about this tree; it stood alone, surrounded by bushes. Bizarrely, the trunk of this giant tree had, at some time in the not-so-distant past, been struck by lightning and had had its upper half burnt out. The breadth of the tree appeared large enough to accommodate a small car. Just below the burnt top, on either side, were two big branches, which grew horizontally and straight till their very ends, where they ramified into multiple twigs like a witch's worn-out broom. A few leaves sprouted from the tip of these small branches. The young man gazed at the tree and winced; he then turned and looked around. The monster's ugliness was in sharp contrast to the beauty of its surroundings. In this oasis of natural beauty, the tree was a misfit.

The path then went past a swimming pool, where a lone swimmer, a girl in her teens, was doing laps. As agile as a dolphin, she dived and tumble-turned for her next lap at the far end of the pool.

Beyond the pool, the path led past the hospital car park and entered the pathology lab through a side entrance.

The pathology lab itself was a small two-storey building that stood next to the much larger main hospital complex and was connected to it by corridors and bridges. Before stepping into the building, the young doctor glanced at his friend, Mr. Cobar, the mountain. The morning sun glistened on the top of the mountain, and he appeared cheerful. Raj thought he could see a flicker of approval on Mr. Cobar's face.

"So far so good," Mr. Cobar appeared to be telling him.

Raj entered the pathology building and was directed to the histopathology department. He walked through the corridor towards his new office. As he neared the office, he saw Dr. Stich running towards him, panting. In his left hand, he clutched a can of fly spray. Raj could not help noticing that the elderly pathologist's fingers were podgy. Raj recalled the saying from Kerala, "Thieves have podgy fingers."

"The flies come from the morgue below." Dr. Stich paused between words to catch his breath. Raj nodded in agreement, for he was learning that he had to agree with everything the elderly pathologist said, did, or thought. Sarah, the office secretary, solemnly told Raj later that Dr. Stich considered flies as his enemy number two, enemy number one being Christians.

Middle aged, medium built, and sprightly, Sarah was great. She knew what to say when and when to say what.

"Dr. Stich recently acquired this deadly weapon," she explained. Sarah would always wink her left emerald-green eye when she talked about Dr. Stich. Her face showed her age with a few creases, but the creases were in the right places. They showed that she smiled often and that she generally had a happy disposition.

"What deadly weapon?" Raj was curious.

"The fly spray—after he swallowed a fly while inhaling for a sneeze. Before that, he only had a fly swat. Dr. Stich had to fight for months with the lab manager, James, before he got the funds for the spray." Sarah suppressed a smile when she narrated the story behind the spray. When she talked, Sarah nodded, as was her custom, and then her straight black hair, which told of southern European descent, would spill over her shoulders.

Sarah had a medium-sized thin nose and a chin that conveyed her determination. Though her chin would seem prominent on another face, it fitted well on hers and only increased her bright demeanour. At five feet seven inches, she was tall and was always dressed in tropical summer clothes—brightly coloured blouses and skirts. Having been born in Australia, she spoke Aussie English. Her grandfather was Italian and had immigrated to Australia after being recruited for the Snowy River project.

Nobody was sure why Dr. Stich considered Christians as his number-one enemy.

"They started all the wars in the world," Dr. Stich once said. Whether that was the reason for his animosity towards Christians, Raj could not say.

As a registrar, Raj's main job was doing the cut-up—in other words, taking pieces from specimens for microscopic examination. The specimens ranged from skin biopsies to gastric and bowel biopsies to resections of stomachs, bowels, or breasts. During cut-up, Raj would dictate the gross or macroscopic appearance of the specimens into a Dictaphone, which Sarah would later type into the pathology report. At the cut-up bench, Raj was assisted by one of the technicians, who would put the pieces Raj had selected to be examined into small cassettes. These were then processed overnight in a tissue-processing machine that would dehydrate the tissue and perfuse it with an organic solvent called xylene.

In the morning the tissue pieces were embedded in wax and manually cut into four to six micron sections using a special cutting machine called a microtome. These sections were then put on a glass slide and stained. The stained sections reached Raj's office by about ten in the morning.

In stage two of the process, Raj would look at the slides under a microscope and also dictate his report into a Dictaphone. Sarah would then type up the report and print the young doctor a copy. He would then take the slides to Dr. Stich, and they would look at them together under a multiheaded microscope, following which the elderly pathologist would make some alterations to the pathology report. Sarah would then type the alterations and print the final report, which would then be signed and sent off to the referring clinician.

Dr. Stich usually reached his office at around nine thirty in the morning, always carrying an elegant black briefcase. He blamed the congested Broome highways for being late. He then spent an hour online reading the news from around the world. All the interesting news he passed onto Raj and Sarah, which was the usual routine at morning tea.

He would also relate to them the escapades of his younger days.

"You know, I wanted to be a do-gooder in India. During one of my travels, I stopped on the banks of the Ganges. I bought a book called *Learn Hindi in Ten Days.* Then I put all my belongings, including my passport, in a locker and went to bed at the railway-station platform, with the book as my pillow. I woke up the next morning to find that the book had disappeared. I went to get my belongings, but the clerk at the locker said that my brother had collected my things an hour earlier. I then decided that Indians did not deserve me."

Raj wanted to tell him that Indians breathed easier that day, but he kept quiet.

"In Baghdad, they chased me to rape me," he continued. Raj doubted that very much, for he could not bring himself to believe that anybody would think of raping Dr. Stich.

"In Pakistan, they thought I was a CIA agent. The India-Pakistan war was about to begin. I had to hide in a hospital for three weeks and escape in an ambulance."

Dr. Stich always stood in the doorway when he made these disclosures. Raj did not know why he liked to stand in that particular spot. Perhaps he did not know that Indians do not like standing in doorways. Many Indians would never stand in a doorway or accept money or greet or shake hands or even talk while standing in a doorway. Raj did have an explanation for this, though he was not exactly sure if it was the right explanation. It was, so he thought, because of Hiranyakasipu, a Hindu mythological character of the ancient Indian texts.

Hiranyakasipu received a boon from Lord Brahma that no man or animal could kill him during the day or night, inside or outside his house, with any weapon. After receiving the boon, Hiranyakasipu boasted that he could do anything without retribution and started harming the gods so much so that the gods complained to Lord Vishnu, who incarnated himself as a creature called Narasimha, which was half man and half animal. Narasimha killed Hiranyakasipu with his bare hands, ripping his chest open with his nails and drinking his blood. He slew him at dusk when it was neither day nor night while standing in the doorway, which was neither inside nor outside the house.

"Maybe that is why most Indians do not like people standing in doorways," Raj thought. He did not tell Dr. Stich about Hiranyakasipu.

The young Indian doctor liked Dr. Stich because he was well known. On Sarah's prompting, Raj researched him on the Internet. He was the author of around 150 articles in peer-reviewed journals, a member of several professional bodies, and the chair of a few of them. At clinical meetings, the surgeons held him in high regard, and now this man was almost calling it a day. Here was this great pathologist leading the idyllic life of semiretirement, at the same time sharing his immense knowledge to his disciples.

Dr. Stich's enemy number three was Mr. James Cabin, the lab manager. James was an Anglo-Indian, and his office was bigger than Dr. Stich's. If Dr. Stich saved money by cutting his own hair, James saved it by not cutting his hair at all. His sideburns were long and reached well below the level of his ears, his eyebrows were bushy, and his hair curled at the nape of his neck and at the bottom of his long sideburns. James had an aquiline nose and slightly protuberant upper and lower jaws. Raj was convinced that James was the reincarnation of the monkey king Hanuman of Hindu mythology.

James had a microscope in his office.

"He needs it to look at his manhood," Dr. Stich told Raj.

James always referred to Dr. Stich as "that dickhead."

That evening Dr. Stich took Raj shopping. The huge malls were different from the tiny shops in India. He showed Raj the cheapest bargains, the shelves where the home-brand products were kept, and the freezer where Ingham whole chicken pieces were stored.

The beautiful mall and streets stood in sharp contrast to the streets in India. Raj recalled the streets in Madras, nowadays called Chennai, which the public also used as toilets. Early morning at five thirty, the streets were so littered with human excrement that one could not walk without stepping on night soil. By eight in the morning, the burning equatorial sun had already changed the shit into solidifying putty, and by ten the traffic had pasted the lumps, in various designs, onto the road. By two in the afternoon, the dry excrement was pulverised into thousands of molecules, which escaped into the air, thanks to the traffic and the dry heat. The smell of the air also changed along with the constitution of the excrement. In the morning the streets reeked of fresh excrement, and in the evening the smell of dry excrement, mixed with the aroma of deep fried samosas and *jalebis*, greeted the public—but the roads were clean. Next day the whole cycle repeated itself. The young man could not but marvel at its cost effectiveness and efficiency, which clearly surpassed the millions of dollars the Australian government put into waste disposal.

Dr. Stich dropped Raj off at his unit after they'd had dinner at Mrs. Singh's curry house. He was tired by the time he reached home and slowly drifted into sleep.

Raj was walking on the path to the hospital from his unit in the middle of the night. There was not a star in sight, but there was a strange glow on the horizon. There, silhouetted in the glow, he could see his friend, Benjora, the mountain. Raj looked down for a moment and then looked at his friend again. Benjora appeared to be gazing at him, but this time, the mountain had the face of a lion and the body of a man, the powerful bloodthirsty Narasimha of Hindu mythology. In his left hand, Narasimha held a struggling man, and with his claws he dug into the chest of the poor wretch. Raj screwed his eyes to see the man's face, but the face was not clearly visible. With a roar, Narasimha tore out the man's heart and lifted it to his face. Blood gushed from the heart, and the beast opened its mouth to suck the blood, which spilt onto his face and ran down his neck.

Suddenly there was a high-pitched scream and a thud.

Raj woke with a start, drenched in sweat. There was shouting coming from outside the room. The young doctor staggered to his feet, walked to the window, and opened the blinds. The lawn outside was well lit from the streetlights surrounding it, illuminating a group of kids playing cricket. The night was cool because of the rain, and Raj had left the windows open. It was around half past nine, and the sounds of the kids playing cricket irritated Raj. "Damn kids, aren't they ever going home?" The young doctor swore in Malayalam, closed the window, and put the air conditioner back on. He lay down, turned his back away from the window, and covered his ears with a pillow. He might have been awake for at least another hour before he finally fell asleep.

CHAPTER 4

THE LAB

The next day, Dr. Stich led Raj on a tour of the department, as he hadn't seen it all on day one. The specimen-processing room was a hall next to the offices of the pathologists and the registrars. All four scientists were of different nationalities by birth. A middle-aged portly, jovial Caucasian man named David was the chief scientist and the only male member in the division of anatomical pathology; the others included a Vietnamese lady in her late forties, a Lebanese girl in her early twenties, and an Eritrean girl in her early thirties. They all said hello to Raj, and Raj, in turn, beamed at them, amused at seeing a kaleidoscopic view of the world in a small lab.

There was a door at the far end of the specimen-processing room, which led to the stores where the specimens were kept until they were destroyed after the pathologists authorised their results. Raj entered the first store, about the size of an office cubicle. He looked around with wonder at shelf after shelf of small jars containing what looked like wrinkled skin. Raj paused and picked up a jar to read the label.

"Those are sacred—put them down," a curt yet sweet voice said behind him. Raj turned to face the Eritrean girl, Maria, and, to his dismay, found himself staring at her. To say that she was beautiful was an understatement; the young lady looked like the descendent of the unholy alliance between Queen Sheba and King Solomon. She was tall and slim, about five foot eight, and looked much younger than her thirty-four years. Raj was sure she was Delilah, the temptress who seduced Samson.

"They belong to the indigenous people. We have to store these foreskins till they collect them when their owners die, and then they are buried with the owners."

Raj looked bemused at the largest collection of foreskins in the world. Over the past fifty years, the lab had collected over twenty thousand foreskins, because it was illegal to throw them away. They had to be held till collected by the next of kin for burial along with the rest of the body, but most were forgotten and were not collected. Their owners had long since departed without their foreskins and were hence unwhole, but the lab still could not throw them away without permission, and they did not know the whereabouts of the relatives. Two storerooms were set apart for these orphaned foreskins, and two pages in the lab manual dealt extensively with their preservation and care.

The girl left and Raj watched her swaying backside. When she passed the door, she paused, turned, and smiled mischievously at Raj. The dusky young doctor smiled back as though mesmerised.

"C'mon!" Dr. Stich called to Raj. There was impatience and urgency in his order. He had obviously noticed his registrar leering at his lady scientist and did not like it.

Raj then passed into the autopsy room escorted by his boss.

Mortui vivos docebunt—*the dead shall teach the living*—was written in a bold Latin alphabet across the main wall. The autopsy room itself was divided in two by a screen, the first for forensic autopsies and the second for medical autopsies. As a histopathologist, Raj was not involved in forensic autopsies, but he could not resist looking at the body on the postmortem table.

A man of about twenty-five years stared back at Raj with his right eye. The left eye and the left half of his face had been replaced with a deep gorge that ended at the left temple, from where brains spilt out like spaghetti. The man's mouth was screwed up in a half scowl, and the protruding tongue drooled, forming a small pool of spit on the floor. The smell of gunpowder and burnt flesh lingered in the air, suggesting that the ghastly incident had taken place less than an hour ago.

"Suicide by a high-powered rifle with the trigger pulled by the toe," Raj diagnosed at first glance. "A representative of Australian youth, who have one of the highest suicide rates in the developed world." Raj wondered what could have led the young man to this gory end. "Maybe a lonely, lovelorn farmer from the vast and dry Aussie plains."

The young doctor's boss led him past the autopsy room to the lab office. There were two funny-looking men there, one sitting at a desk and the other standing next to him, both looking very serious and staring at the computer. Like grandmasters at a world chess championship, they appeared deeply engrossed in solving a most difficult problem.

To Raj, these characters were straight out of the pages of Tintin comics. In his mind he dubbed them Thomson and Thompson, after the bumbling, bald headed, moustachioed detectives. The men shared an uncanny resemblance both to each other and to the characters themselves.

"Meet Jack and Frank," Dr. Stich introduced them to Raj, who extended his hand to Jack, the man who was standing. Jack shook his hand half-heartedly.

"We will go back to our office," Dr. Stich said, cutting short the meeting before it had even started. During the walk back, Dr. Stich gave a concise description of the two technicians.

He told Raj that the two were not related, but ever since fate had brought them together, they had stuck together like a pair of twins. Jack Heath was an army reservist, who had grown up in the Outback in foster homes. He had his first experience with drugs when he was twelve. By the time he was thirteen, he was growing pot in his backyard, and by fifteen he was selling high-quality pot, soon graduating to heroin. Although Mr. Heath sold heroin, he never used it. He was arrested and sent for rehabilitation, following which he turned over a new leaf. He became a butcher and completed a diploma in medical science from TAFE. Through hard work and determination, Jack studied nursing, becoming a psychiatric nurse and a forensic technician by the age of thirty-five.

Jack was bisexual and lived with his Filipino wife and their five-and three-year-old sons, to whom Jack was a good father; he spent a lot of time with them. He also had three children from an early liaison, but they lived with their mother.

Jack was of medium height, five foot nine, with a stocky build and the thick neck of a boxer. A broken nose from a fistfight during his youth complemented his face. His eyebrows were represented by a few scattered bristles, which made him look almost browless. His jaw receded slightly. A thick vein started from the outer edge of his left eyebrow and curved across his forehead before climbing to and disappearing at the summit of his completely bald head that he shaved regularly every morning to remove the occasional lone hair.

Nobody knew much about the personal life of Frank Witherspoon, the other autopsy technician, who lived by himself. Apart from being Jack's colleague and confidant, there was nothing much known about him. He was bald, like his friend, but slightly taller, about six feet, and his thin body made him look a bit taller than his actual height. Frank always wore long-sleeved shirts and long trousers. He had joined the forensic department ten years earlier.

Four forensic pathologists had joined and left in a short time, giving rise to several rumours about their arrivals and early exits.

Jack and Frank were the kings of the autopsy room and the fridge where the bodies were kept. During the day the orderlies were allowed to put bodies in the fridge without the permission of the technicians, but after hours, only the autopsy technicians had the authority to do this, and hence one of them had to be on call every night. The two thus made a fortune working overtime, and since they preferred nights to days and death to life, they were known among the hospital staff as "dark angels."

Raj saw the autopsy technicians once more that day when they came to the histopathology lab for something. Raj was in the corridor on the way to his office when they passed him, walking abreast and talking to each other seriously. Jack and Frank glanced at Raj, but they did not bother to greet him, instead giving him a mocking smile, a smile such of the kind the visiting American secretary of state would reserve for the Indian slums as his motorcade sped from the airport to the Rajbhavan—the official residence of the Indian president.

CHAPTER 5

RAJ

Bhagyvandhom prasooyedha, ma
sooram, ma cha panditham.
("Give birth to the fortunate, not to the
courageous or the learned.")

That night Raj found it difficult to sleep. There was something
scary about this place, which he was not able to pinpoint.

Was it the autopsy technicians?

Was it the ugly lightning-struck tree?

Was it Dr. Stich?

The young man's mind wandered to his childhood. He remembered the advice that Kunthi, the mother of the five Pandavas brothers, had given Panchali, their wife and her own daughter-in-law, in the great Hindu epic, *Mahabharata*: "Bhagyvandhom prasooyedha, ma sooram, ma cha panditham" ("Give birth to the fortunate, not to the courageous or the learned.")

Raj was sure that his mother had not given birth to the courageous or the learned or even the fortunate. As a boy he was not courageous, for he was scared of the dark and of heights; nor was he learned or fortunate. He was sure that if he were fortunate, he would have become an actor.

Raj's acting career died even before it was born. The boy was in year three in primary school when his young and pretty class teacher asked him to audition for a character for the annual school play. Three or four of the other teachers were also there in the staffroom eagerly waiting for their protégé to audition. The teacher read out the role for the boy to act, but as he was about to start, to his horror of horrors, the young boy saw that his underwear lace was sneaking out from below the bottom of his shorts. Raj hid the lace with his left hand, gently rolling it and holding it under his shorts. The role was that of a stern policeman, but to the consternation of the young ladies, this particular policeman was acting very strangely; there was an embarrassed look on the officer's face, and the harsh words came out as a weak stammer. Instead of gesticulating with both hands, the policeman was using only one hand, the other hand nervously holding on to his shorts.

"You can go back to the classroom." There was disappointment and bewilderment on the teachers' faces.

Raj never told anybody the reason for the failure of his acting career.

Throughout his life, the young doctor was very absent-minded, and he sincerely believed that absent-mindedness equated with intelligence, as most great scientists were absent-minded. He conveniently forgot that the reverse—that most absent-minded people were great scientists—was not true.

Once and only once did Raj think that he had found somebody more absent-minded than himself. It happened during an incident that occurred while he was working as a general practitioner in a small town in Kerala.

It might have been seven at night when he visited the computer school to meet one of his friends who worked there. As they often did when they entered revered places in India, Raj left his shoes outside the school office before sitting down to talk. While they were talking, the power went off, which, again, was not unusual in that part of the world, and Raj and the computer teacher continued their conversation in candlelight.

Suddenly there was a knock on the door.

"Can you do this work for me?" The stranger at the door puffed as he made the request between deep breaths; he obviously wanted to get something typed in a jiffy. But there was no power, so the computer teacher declined to do the job, and the man went off into the darkness as suddenly as he had appeared at the door.

After their meeting, the young doctor stepped outside the office to find an odd pair of shoes there: a leather sandal and a rubber thong.

"Son of a bitch," he swore, "I hope he soon realises what he has done and comes back to return my sandal and take back his worn-out thong. Surely he won't like wearing an odd pair of shoes." The young doctor was angry at the stranger who had walked away with one of his good sandals.

Raj then walked back to his house, trying to keep to the shadows, for the people at Kolenchery, the small town where he practised, were not used to seeing their doctor walking barefooted. When he reached home, to his shock, Raj found an odd pair of shoes matching the ones at the computer school; it seemed it was he who had been lost in his thoughts again, and at that very moment, the young man gave up trying to find somebody more absent-minded than himself.

Raj abhorred many of the conveniences of modern society, because he believed that these conveniences had a way of backfiring. For example, he did not like sunglasses, because, to him, they were barriers to communication. "People express themselves with their eyes; even the blind smile with their eyes," Raj reasoned. "If one cannot see the other person's expression, how can we communicate with him? Strangers on the road, even if they do not talk to each other, communicate with their eyes. Sunglasses have stopped all that."

The young doctor particularly disliked the motorcar. He would say, "Back home, people met each other at bus stops. The crowded buses were the places where people met their friends and socialised daily in a very informal manner. Cocooned in the car, the modern man does not know who his neighbour is; he knows only the route he takes to his work. He does not see the lily on the roadside, nor does he see the riot of colours the bougainvillaea creates: the modern man sees them only in the pictures that adorn his office walls."

Raj did not think much of the television or the computer either. "These great inventions for communication separate people instead of bringing them closer."

As a medical student, the young man was a stirrer, though he never meant to be. It was in his genes, and that was certainly why the girls did not like him at the medical school during his training for his MBBS. Raj knew that it was because of his reputation that they left him out at the annual ladies' hostel dinner at Calicut Medical School, for they had invited everybody else in their batch but him.

Raj decided he had to be there for the dinner, invitation or no invitation. Luckily for him, the men's hostel secretary, Chakravarthy, was his friend and agreed to be his accomplice.

The evening of the dinner, the young stirrer carried a ladder to the ladies' hostel and leaned it against the first-floor balcony adjacent to the dining hall. Soon Raj was sitting on the ladies' hostel balcony, wearing his sarong—or lungi, as the colourful loincloth is known—feasting on chapatti, the flat Indian bread, and fish curry.

The dinner had started in the hall adjacent to the balcony. The distinguished guests, including the principal of the medical school, had arrived.

"Shall we open the window and let in some fresh, cool breeze?" suggested Raj's friend Chakravarthy. Vidya, the ladies' hostel secretary, agreed and drew the blinds, and there in full view of the august crowd was the lonely medical student in his lungi, enjoying his chapatti.

The door to the balcony opened, and Raj heard an attractive voice ask, "Why don't you join us?" And that is how he met Vidya.

Raj indeed took the spotlight that night, dining and dancing and entertaining the crowd in the most inappropriate dress.

Something stirred in Vidya's heart that night. Was it that Vidya liked Raj's simplicity, honesty, and humility? Raj liked the simple things in life—cold lemonade on a hot day was his greatest enjoyment; so was the common chickpea curry and *puttu* (a dish made of rice flour) steamed in a pipe. Raj also relished *idlies* (cakes made of steamed rice and lentil).

One of his greatest heroes was the American president Theodore Roosevelt. "I preach not the doctrine of ignoble ease, but the doctrine of strenuous life" was one of Raj's favourite quotes.

How can he, the unlucky, the noncourageous, extremely absent-minded, and fun-loving doctor from a village in a third-world country survive here? What merits did he have? True, he had an MBBS and a pathology postgraduate degree from truly wonderful institutions, but India was still India, and degrees from India were still Indian degrees.

Though he did not relish the tropical climate, Broome was beautiful; there was no doubt about that. The hospital was well kept, and the lab was orderly and well organised, yet there was something odd somewhere. In this oasis of beauty, there were things that did not match or fit. Dr. Stich was extremely good at pathology, but why was he wasting his intelligence here? What was he doing in Broome? Pathologists aged slowly, and at Dr. Stich's age, they were in their prime. What vested interest did he have in Broome? And how did Thomson and Thompson, the autopsy technicians, survive here? They not only survived but also seemed to thrive. Sarah the secretary and Maria the Eritrean scientist, both of whom exemplified the beauty and goodness of the world, too seemed misfits here, although they acted as though they belonged.

The young doctor missed his wife terribly. She was the strength behind him. Though a quiet person, her courage in adverse situations had seen them withstand difficult times. Raj had rung her unit at nine that night, but there was no answer, and her mobile was switched off. In the end, he rang the lab at the Royal Adelaide Hospital, and his guess was correct: his wife was there at nine in the night, working long hours to complete her project.

"I'm doing fine," Vidya said, but she did not sound fine on the phone. Though tired, Vidya wanted to finish the project she was handling and leave for Broome to be with Raj. They had lived together ever since they had married two years ago, but now they were physically separated, and she was feeling lonely. Raj too tried to hide his feelings of loneliness and the strangeness of the place by telling her that he was okay, but his wife sensed a lack of enthusiasm in his voice even though, when she questioned him, he assured her it was nothing to worry about.

"How is your project going?" the young pathologist asked his wife.

"It's okay. I might be able to finish it in about six months instead of one year as I had thought." There was a sigh of relief.

"Bye, and please have a good night."

"Good night to you too." She blew a kiss into the phone.

"Kiss you too."

Raj hung up, misty-eyed. His mind again wandered to his prospects in the harsh Aussie weather and the harsher circumstances he appeared to be in.

"Not courageous, not fortunate, not learned. What can sustain me? Honesty, maybe."

Raj was as honest as the day was long. "But would that be enough? Would honesty be an asset here or a drawback? Belief, maybe. The Lord of Moses, who guided the Israelites through the desert, will guide me. Jesus, who died for me, who begs with His Father all the time to give me one more chance in spite of my weaknesses, may help me."

Raj said a short prayer. After that, his mind became a bit clearer, and he soon drifted off to sleep.

CHAPTER 6

VIDYA

She was a phantom of delight.

—Wordsworth

Separated by thousands of kilometres, Raj slowly began to realize what Vidya had meant to him.

He recalled Wordsworth's poem: "She was a phantom of delight." Was the great poet describing his own wife or every wife in the world when he wrote this? Or did he foresee what Raj's wife was going to be, many, many years ago? From an ethereal beauty at the time of their courtship, Vidya had emerged as a source of strength, "a spirit, yet a woman too." She was tall, around five feet seven, and exceptionally pretty. It was not enough to say that she was beautiful. Vidya looked like a goddess sculpted from East Indian Rosewood.

While they were dating, Vidya took Raj to her house in Vadakara, an hour's journey by bus from their medical school. Vidya's father was a commander in the Indian Army and was posted in Kashmir.

He lived in the barracks with her mother and a younger brother who went to high school there.

Vidya's house at Vadakara was a huge *nalukettu* (a house with a central courtyard), where her grandmother, Yesodhayamma, lived with two servants: a maid to look after her personal needs and a male housekeeper. She was partially blind and deaf, but her intelligence was sharp, and age had not diminished her memory.

Vidya knocked on the door.

"Who is that?" the old lady asked from inside.

"Me, Vidya."

"Come in."

Vidya beckoned Raj inside the house. They left their shoes outside and entered the living room, which was huge and opened into the central courtyard.

"Come here," the old lady called from the room on the left.

Vidya's grandmother was reclining on her bed and cooling herself with a palm-leaf fan.

"Grandma, how are you?" Vidya greeted her politely.

"Who is that?" Although age had diminished her eyesight, Yesodhayamma could see that Vidya was not alone.

"My friend."

"Your friend?"

"Yes."

"I did not know you had a friend like this."

"Well..."

"What is his name?"

In conservative Kerala, girls were not supposed to have boyfriends.

"Raj."

"Does your daddy know?"

"Yes."

Yesodhayamma knew this was a lie, but she had been a young girl once and understood.

"Give him something to drink."

Raj exchanged pleasantries with Yesodhayamma, who appeared tired and did not talk a lot, and the young couple withdrew into the living room. Vidya then took her boyfriend to the room on the right, a fairly large bedroom with a large window and a door that opened to the outside.

"This is my room."

Gazing out of the window, Raj could see a long shed with a low thatched roof.

"What is that?"

"Come with me."

Vidya opened an almirah in the bedroom and took out a bunch of keys. Raj accompanied his girlfriend outside the house to the shed. She unlocked the door and led Raj down a flight of mud steps to the floor below. The shed was a dug-out rectangular pit in the ground, the walls of which were actually the surrounding earth, as was the floor. There were weapons, swords, daggers, maces, and lances piled in the left corner and against the wall, at the far end of the shed.

"Copy what I do," Vidya said.

The young lady walked to the far left corner and stood before the sharp metal weapons. She bent down. As a sign of reverence, she touched the ground with her right hand, after which she touched her own forehead with the same hand. Raj copied her way of paying obeisance.

Vidya then took a curved sword and a small shield from the pile and, turning towards her boyfriend, said, "Move to one side."

The weapons had given her unusual power, and Vidya's voice sounded authoritative, which made the young man instinctively obey her and move closer to the wall. Vidya suddenly started executing movements of *kalari*, the ancient martial art of Kerala. She kicked in the air with her right foot and then squatted on the same foot, followed by a leap into the air and a simultaneous swirling of her sword.

Raj walked to the corner where the weapons were kept and selected a lance and shield from the pile. He saluted the gods, the same way his girlfriend had, and then turned around and faced Vidya. It was the young lady's turn to be surprised.

"*Marapiduchu kuntham*," she murmured.

"Yeah, I too grew up in Kerala. I started practising kalari when I was five."

"Take off your shirt."

Raj obeyed his warrior girlfriend's command and unbuttoned his shirt. Men had to be bare breasted when practising kalari.

"Take your shirt off," he said.

Women were allowed to wear a top when practising kalari, but Raj was trying his luck with Vidya, and he was rewarded when the young lady, without a word, put her weapons on the floor and took her T-shirt off, her breasts heaving within her bra.

What followed was a high-calibre exposition of warfare from ancient Kerala. The warriors executed gravity-defying leaps; their swords slashed, and their lances thrust with lightning speed, and sparks flew when the weapons clashed with each other. The air was filled with the whoosh and clang of weapons and beads of perspiration from the warriors' bodies. Finally, tired after about half an hour, the young couple put their weapons down and stood for a moment facing each other in the dim light of the setting sun that percolated through the thatched roof, sweat streaking down their glistening bodies. A drop of sweat wandered into the cleavage between Vidya's breasts.

Vidya suddenly executed a sweep with her right foot, and before he realised it, Raj was on the floor on his back. The girl then leapt in the air and landed on Raj's chest lightly, like a cat; in a moment she had reached behind and taken off her bra, her perfect breasts quivering in the fading light. The young girl lay on top of

Raj on the mud floor and kissed him, at first gently and then with increasing passion.

They made love that night on the kalari floor, watched by the gods.

Ten minutes later they were lying side by side, panting and exhausted. Raj pulled Vidya back on top of him, and sweat dripped from their naked bodies onto the mud. She rested her face on his chest, and tears flowed from her eyes.

"I love you," she said quietly.

"I love you too," Raj replied.

They lay like that for about another ten minutes. The lovers then slowly got up and put their clothes on over their sweaty and muddy bodies, following which they walked out of the shed and back to the house. Yesodhayamma was asleep by then. Raj stayed in the living room, but Vidya went to the kitchen and had a brief chat with the maid before they left. It was ten in the night when they arrived back at the medical school. The young man escorted his girlfriend to her hostel and gave her a long good-night kiss.

CHAPTER 7

THE FIRST WEEK

The first week passed slowly.

"The first week always passes slowly," Raj philosophised, "after which, time seems to fly, so if one wants to age slowly, one should keep changing jobs every week. But then, changing jobs would become routine, and time would start flying again."

Most evenings Dr. Stich went shopping, not because he bought a lot of things but because he did not buy a lot of things. The elderly doctor would go to the prettiest girl at the counter and ask, "Why don't you sell home-brand mineral water? Why is your Ingham chicken dearer by twenty cents a kilo?" At first the girls thought that Dr. Stich was slightly strange, but they soon accepted him and appreciated how he helped them while away the time. He was a welcome interlude during their monotonous evening routines.

Friday arrived, and there was Dr. Stich at the doorway at five o'clock in the evening. "Come with me" was the command. His blue eyes were cheerful, for it was Friday evening, a day on which happy hour in the pubs ran later than usual.

Dr. Stich would visit most of the pubs during happy hour for the free chicken wings the barmaids took around. He also did not think it was unbecoming to lean over and help himself to nibbles from the plate of a stranger, who would look up in surprise but would then accept this odd interference with cheerful submission. Raj also used to be startled in the beginning at the unusual behaviour of his boss but later got used to it and found his quaint habits quite amusing.

On one occasion he told Raj, "Twenty years ago there was a great fire at the hospital, in the pathology department. After it was contained, I went around salvaging the books." Dr. Stich showed Raj those books with their edges singed.

Raj and Dr. Stich found a place amid the din.

"I had my own bar here twenty years ago," Dr. Stich told Raj on one occasion. "My bar was next to the gay club; the bishop of Broome was the most frequent visitor to the gay club."

A short, medium-built elderly man with bushy eyebrows and thinning hair separated himself from the crowd at the bar and drifted towards them. He had the expression of a boy who was about to cry.

"I have been sleeping better these days," he said.

"That is fantastic," Dr. Stich replied and, turning to Raj, said, "Meet Don—Don Coward. He's our local member of parliament."

Dr. Stich then tried to introduce Raj to Don, but even though he took a seat at their table, he looked away. Don studied his wine glass intently and swirled it slowly. He tilted the glass to his nose, smelt it, and inhaled deeply. He then took a small sip, pouting his lips before drawing the corner of his mouth to one side, all the time swirling the wine in his mouth, the bulge of juice appearing in different areas of his left and right cheek. Raj watched this performance in fascination.

Finally, Don drew his lips upwards and said, "There is a faint taste of nutmeg with an aroma of orange—very nice."

Mr. Coward then gave Raj a distrustful look and walked away.

Raj wondered how Don would know the taste of nutmeg so well, for he was certain Don wouldn't have seen a nutmeg or tasted one on its own during his entire life. He thought wistfully of his father's lush tropical garden where nutmeg trees stood among coconut palms and betel nut palms to which pepper vines clung. Raj's father sold the nutmeg at a good price, and he also made a syrupy wine out of the nutmeg fruit.

"Don Coward sleeps badly or gets no sleep at all when he has nightmares, in which Australia appears as a boat in an ocean full of refugees who swim towards it, trying to clamber in, with some clinging to the sides," Dr. Stich explained. "But occasionally Don has good dreams, where he grows very big, like a giant, plucks the refugees from the boat and hand-feeds them to the crocodiles." Dr. Stich paused before continuing, "Crocodiles are an endangered species."

"And human beings are not," Raj muttered to himself. Though he did not quite agree with Dr. Stich, Raj nodded his head.

Dr. Stich's enemy number four was, together, the two autopsy technicians, whom he counted as one, for they were united in daring and deceit. Though their features resembled the twin detectives, Thompson and Thomson, they differed greatly in intelligence from the famously inept cartoon characters of yesteryear. These guys were not just intelligent, if one were to use the proper words. Instead, they were extremely cunning and clever.

"Jack and Frank, the autopsy technicians, wield great power; the coroner is on their side. Many forensic pathologists have come and gone, falling victim to the system. The last victim was Dr. Dumbbell. He was honest and tried to fight them. Finally, the stress made him mad." Dr. Stich went on like a running commentary at a footy match. Suddenly he paused and, craning his head towards Raj, said in a hissing voice, "Dr. Dumbbell committed suicide. They found him hanging from the large lightning-struck eucalyptus tree."

Raj was startled and drew back as though by instinct. He felt sick and excused himself. He staggered to his feet and ambled to the toilet, where he threw up.

"Is it Delhi belly?" Dr. Stich enquired when he returned.

Dr. Stich usually dropped Raj off at home after these evening outings, but that day the older man had to go home earlier than usual for some reason, and the younger man caught the bus to the hospital, where he got off and started walking to his unit. He was midway between the hospital and his unit when there was a sudden gust of wind, accompanied by sheets of rain. A tree branch must have fallen on the power lines, for the power went out, and Raj found himself in pitch darkness. Lightning streaked across the sky, and in that light that lingered for a moment, Raj saw a glimpse of the giant eucalyptus tree again, which looked eerily different that night. The gaping hole at the top of the main trunk produced by a previous lightning strike looked like a huge mouth and the two huge branches on either side of the hole were like large arms on each side of the ghastly maw. In the wind, the arms swayed towards Raj as if to snatch him.

Raj was drenched by the time he reached his quarters. He started shivering; was it the cold, or was it something else, a strange fear that he could not explain?

From that night onwards, Raj took a circuitous route from the bus stop to his unit, well away from the lightning-struck eucalyptus tree.

CHAPTER 8

ARRIVAL OF IQBAAL

In spite of his eccentric behaviour, Dr. Stich appeared to be the friendliest boss in the world. Apart from helping the young doctor settle down, he relied on Raj for everything, such as acting as an intermediary between himself and the lab staff, including talking to James, the lab manager. Come weekends they would visit Broome's various beaches and bars, or Dr. Stich would seek Raj's help at his cashew-nut farm, where he helped the elderly pathologist prune and fertilise the cashew trees.

The farm was spread over one hundred acres and was situated an hour's drive from the hospital. A neighbouring farmer took care of the trees, which had started to yield fruit. Dr. Stich said he grew cashews because of his love for India and everything that came from it. He exported the dried nuts to India for further processing.

"I visit the farm routinely so that they know I am keeping an eye on it," the elderly pathologist explained.

That hot and humid Saturday, the two pathologists arrived at the cashew farm at around eleven in the morning. Both men quickly stripped to their waists, got out the pruning scissors and saws, and started working. Soon they were drenched in sweat, and within a couple of hours, Raj started to tire. But Dr. Stich kept on working with amazing speed and dexterity in spite of his apparent lack of fitness.

"Dog tired I am," said Raj to himself. "And this man, who does not look half as healthy as I am, is going like a steam engine with no plans of stopping." To stop and rest would be admitting defeat to a potbellied, unfit elderly man, so the younger man kept on going until, to his immense relief, Dr. Stich decided to call it a day. They put their shirts on, and the young doctor accompanied his boss to his neighbour's house, where three beefy men, a middle-aged farmer and his two boys in their early twenties, were drinking beer and watching television after their morning's labour.

"Howyougoin?" They shook Raj's hand and greeted him in their Australian one-worded but three-syllabled expression.

"How are you?" Raj returned the pleasantries, for he had not yet learnt the art of saying "how are you going" in one word and hence preferred to keep to the simpler way of greeting.

"Raj Thomas works with me. He came to help me today," Dr. Stich explained. The big Aussie men nodded approvingly at the small black Indian.

"I am not small in India," Raj thought. "Each one of these guys is twice my size." Compared to these giants, he was puny, and Raj felt their size intimidating and their manners reproachable. The Aussie blokes did not offer Raj a drink, but Raj was given ice-cold water after asking for some.

On the way back, they stopped at a bar in a country town. The twentysomething barmaids wore ultra miniskirts, and Raj stared lustfully at their long, pale legs.

"Do you want to fuck her?"

Raj was startled at the abrupt and rude remark of the middle-aged male bartender.

"They are very rough people," Dr. Stich reminded Raj as they walked to the car.

A few months after Raj's arrival, Dr. Stich employed a locum pathologist from Saudi Arabia for two months to report routine cases while Dr. Stich took on a research project. He said he had to catch up with some important scientific work.

"Dr. Iqbaal Mehammood is a great pathologist," Dr. Stich began the introduction two days before Iqbaal's arrival. "He's a world leader in liver pathology—especially transplant pathology. The sheikhs of Saudi are his patients. All of them are alcoholics, and they need donor livers to replace their own, which are cirrhotic. The donor livers come from the enemies of Islam and traitors." Dr. Stich squinted at Raj. "The number of these enemies of Islam is directly proportional to the level of alcohol consumption in the palaces."

Raj did not fail to notice the BBC headlines the next day on the Internet: "President Bush praises the House of Saud for their commitment to democracy."

It was Raj's turn to do the airport run, so it was he who picked up Iqbaal from the airport. Iqbaal was tall and gaunt, with his head propped up by a long, thin neck, which might as well have belonged to a giraffe. His body was equally slim, and his walk resembled the slithering of a snake. Iqbaal's well-trimmed beard and moustache, cut well above the lips, certified that he was a practising Muslim and helped Raj to identify him easily. His complexion was that of a Middle Eastern Arab, neither black nor pale, somewhere in between, maybe wheat coloured.

"*As-Salaam-Alaikum*," Iqbaal said, nodding his big head, which was adorned by a big nose and lower jaw that made his head resemble that of a camel.

"*Wa alaykum al-salaam*," Raj replied. Iqbaal was pleased when Raj returned his greetings in Arabic. He looked at Raj and grinned, and his deeply sunk eyes glinted like jewels in a cave.

Iqbaal was very fast with the slides. Every day he would finish the work within two hours and spend the rest of the time on the Internet, trading shares.

The Saudi pathologist prayed five times a day in his office like any pious Muslim.

Raj and Iqbaal went bushwalking the first Saturday after his arrival. First they drove about sixty kilometres in the Land Cruiser that the hospital had lent Iqbaal to drive during his stay in Broome. The Saudi doctor drove carefully, but he kept drifting to the right side of the road, and instead of switching the indicators on, he constantly switched the wipers on, which creaked when they wiped the dusty windscreen. Iqbaal would swear in Arabic before he flicked the wiper switch off.

"In Saudi, right is right," he tried to explain to Raj. "The turning indicator lever and the wiper lever are reversed here."

The sealed road gave way to red mud and the green landscape became thinner, being replaced by shrubs. Iqbaal stopped the car at the start of a bushwalking path, and they got out and read the signs. The Indian doctor then checked the backpacks, making sure they had enough supplies for the two-hour walk they had planned, three litres of water each, a few bars of chocolate, and a flare each if they lost their way. The flares were Raj's idea.

The rugged treeless land was overwhelming in its beauty, which made their trek less tiring than it could have been. Grazing on the brown shrubs were brown kangaroos, which stopped munching and gazed at the two-legged intruders. An hour must have passed since their walk had started, when Iqbaal suddenly headed into the bushes and started searching for something.

"What are you looking for?" Raj shouted.

"A stone," Iqbaal answered.

Finally, the Saudi man found the stone he was looking for, and then he squatted and piddled; when he was done, he carefully blotted the last drop from the tip of his penis with the stone. "All true Muslims do this," Iqbaal explained to Raj. "We squat to piddle, since squatting compresses the bladder and squeezes the last drop of juice out." Iqbaal's long camel-like face became philosophical when he described the science of piddling.

By the time they returned home, Raj was worn out and ready for a couple of Victoria Bitters before dozing off on the couch, which as always was cluttered with books.

Raj was riding a camel, and his buttocks were aching. He was very restless and so was the camel, which had stopped and started looking around as though searching for something. He sniffed the sand and, with his feet, started burrowing the desert as though he was hunting for lost treasure. The bursting pain in Raj's lower abdomen was becoming unbearable. Suddenly the camel threw Raj into the sand and ran towards a large rock on the horizon, on reaching which the animal squatted and piddled in the sand and used the boulder as his blotting stone.

Raj cried out loudly waking as he fell off the couch and his head banged on the floor. He staggered to the toilet, and the urine gushed out like the mighty Nile. Raj mentally thanked the inventor of toilet paper. He took Ackermann's textbook of pathology, on which he was sleeping, and put it on the table and went back to sleep—this time more comfortably in his bed without the huge textbook under him.

CHAPTER 9

THE TURN OF EVENTS

Veliyelirunna pampine eduthu konathi vechamathiri.
("Just like taking a snake that was lying on the
fence and putting it in your underwear.")

On Sunday evening Raj accompanied Iqbaal in his car to the Cable Beach markets. The rains had ceased, and the humidity had given way to the lovely dry season. They parked the car on the extensive lawns near the beach, which had been converted into a huge makeshift car park, from where they had to walk almost a kilometre to reach the markets. The Cable Beach markets were seasonal and consisted of several small shacks trading trinkets and ethnic food, magicians and acrobats entertaining the crowd, soothsayers selling yarns to gullible hippies, and face painters drawing on pretty girls' cheeks. There were a couple of teenage girls in hipsters and bikini tops walking ahead of them and slurping ice-cream cones with kilos of fat yo-yoing on either side of their trouser belts. Although he considered hipsters, along with communism, the cruellest things human beings had ever created, Raj perved at their exposed buttocks when the girls bent to inspect some curios.

Raj and Iqbaal walked around the markets and came across a stall selling leather goods, second-hand radios, audio cassette players, and small televisions. A leather briefcase caught Raj's eye. It was made with soft black leather and was an elegant document carrier. He opened the briefcase; the label on the inside read "Pigskin."

"How much do you want for this?" he asked.

"Thirty dollars," the somewhat middle-aged Chinese vendor said.

"Twenty," Raj replied.

"You Indian?"

"Yes."

"It's yours for twenty-five."

Raj promptly paid the vendor twenty-five dollars, happy that it was his lucky day.

"Dr. Stich has a history," Iqbaal said matter-of-factly as they ate at a place at the markets called Grandma's Fish and Chips. "He came to Broome after they kicked him out of the London Hospital, where he was working."

"What happened?" Raj was curious.

"Well, a lot of things happened when he was the Director of Pathology at the hospital in London. Nobody liked him. All his research is bullshit. There were even criminal cases against him."

Even though Raj tried, Iqbaal would not divulge the details.

The two months of Iqbaal's appointment were coming to a close, and Dr. Stich's working holiday was ending. It was time for Iqbaal to leave. He had become very quiet and spent a lot of time with the hospital administrative director and the pay office, and even when he came to the lab, he did not talk but went gloomily to his office where he quickly finished his work.

One day Raj met David, the chief scientist, in the corridor.

"Raj, I believe Iqbaal has gone mad," David said.

"What happened?"

"He is creating a lot of problems. He's in the administrative office most of the time. He says he did overtime on weekends and is claiming more salary. I reckon he did not know about the taxation in Australia. He was peeved when he was paid and found that almost fifty percent went to the taxman."

"Yeah, in Saudi they don't pay any tax. So did they give him more pay?" Raj was curious.

"No."

Even the day that he left, Iqbaal did not talk and did not even bother to say goodbye to anybody. The taxi arrived, and he got into it and left.

A very relaxed-looking Dr. Stich returned to work afterwards; the elderly pathologist had finished his research project. He invited Raj, Sarah, and Maria to a meeting in his office.

"I am planning to give Iqbaal a permanent position," he said. "What is your opinion? I know he is a somewhat fraudulent character. But I would like to employ a second pathologist."

Raj could not say anything for some time, as he was in a dilemma: should he tell the truth about Iqbaal, how he had gossiped about Dr. Stich, and risk the boss's wrath for divulging secrets about him, or should he give a good report and let the scoundrel enter the Australian workforce? After a lot of deliberation, Raj decided to tell the truth, and as he feared, Dr. Stich did not receive the well-intentioned and honest disclosure well.

From that day there was a dramatic change in Dr. Stich's attitude towards the young doctor. The elderly pathologist's tenderness towards Raj was replaced with intense hatred. Before this incident happened, Dr. Stich's routine was to be at Raj's office at five every evening when he would command Raj to stop for the day and accompany him to various pubs for his evening drinks. The very same day the ill-fated meeting took place, Dr. Stich gave Raj extra work at half past four in the afternoon with an order to finish the work by five. The young doctor hurried through his work and somehow submitted it in time, but the older man found mistakes in everything Raj had done.

"*Sinus* is singular and plural. There is no such word as *sinuses*. Sinus singular is pronounced *sinus*, and sinus plural is pronounced *sinoos*," Dr. Stich thundered, looking at the Indian doctor's pathology reports. "*Tumour* means swelling, in Latin, and does not mean new growth, for which you need to use the term *neoplasm*." The old man started interpreting every medical term according to its literal Latin translation, his former charming quirkiness giving way to madness.

Raj wanted to tell Dr. Stich about the Puri car festival. Raj remembered visiting Puri, in the Indian state of Orissa, with his dad when Raj was a boy. Puri is famous for its festival, where hundreds of thousands of devotees pull the chariot of Lord Jagannaath or Vishnu around the city. For the festival each year, new chariots, almost six stories high, are made using tonnes of hardwood. The huge chariot with the statue of Jagannaath upon it is pulled by thousands of people around the streets of Puri and such is its momentum, that it is almost impossible to stop. Over the years the unstoppable Jagannaath has come to be known as *juggernaut*.

"Dr. Stich does not know that the meaning of words change over the years and that they sometimes mean something quite different from their parent word. *Tumour* in English means new growth and not swelling as it does in Latin," Raj thought. But Raj did not tell Dr. Stich about the Puri car festival or Jagannaath or juggernaut.

That evening Raj walked with a bowed head and hunched shoulders to his unit.

"Honesty does not pay dividends," the Indian doctor said to himself, as he could not quite understand the sudden change in Dr. Stich's attitude towards him. One moment he was the crown prince and second in command of the division of Anatomical

Pathology, and the next he was at the receiving end of a long and hard stick.

"Shouldn't I have told him the truth?" Raj wondered.

"Raj."

The young doctor turned around to face the owner of the sweet and demure voice. Maria hastened towards him. Even during the time of this intense mental torment, Raj couldn't help being transfixed at the Eritrean girl's beauty.

In the twilight her skin glowed like a glass of light black tea. Her slightly curly black hair cascaded to her shoulders, and the setting sun gave it an angelic glow. Her middle was narrow, but her hips were rounded where the silhouette of her buttocks could be seen through her long muslin skirt. She wore white sandals with medium heels, and a gold anklet adorned her left ankle.

Suddenly Raj realised he had been staring at her.

"Yeah, what's up?" he shouted to cover his embarrassment.

The girl walked a little closer. Her haunting brown eyes, though they appeared a bit worried, twinkled and smiled each time Raj caught them. Long eyelashes and long straight eyebrows with pointed outer ends decorated her eyes. Raj could envisage Cupid filing his arrows in a vain attempt to make them as sharp as her eyebrows. She had high cheekbones and a straight nose.

"Maybe it was a mistake," Maria said, a dimple appearing in her left cheek.

"What was a mistake?" Raj could not help noticing that the neck of her blouse was cut low and revealed the cleavage between firm hillocks, the summits of which throbbed beneath her white cotton apparel. His eyes strayed, and for a moment the doctor envied the white teardrop pearl pendant that danced between those hillocks. She had matching white pearl stud earrings, and two rows of perfect white teeth complemented the ornaments.

"You telling Dr. Stich about his past."

"Are you telling me that I should have let him take in that scoundrel?"

"No, you should have told him, but at a different time—not when we were around."

"What difference would that have made?"

"While it is imperative that you should have told Dr. Stich about Iqbaal's true nature, Dr. Stich wouldn't have wanted us to know of his past. You probably should've spoken to him privately about what Iqbaal told you about him."

"You think that is the reason for his change in behaviour?"

"It could be." Though her words were not definite, her tone was sincere. Raj, it seemed, had committed a tactical error for which he would have to pay for the rest of his time there.

"Thank you," Raj said, turning to leave.

"I hope I didn't offend you."

"No, you didn't. On the contrary, you did the right thing by telling me."

The beautiful girl lingered for a moment, and then she slowly walked away.

Raj watched her, and when she was out of sight, he looked towards the setting sun. Mr. Cobar, his mountain friend, was there surveying the things that happened around him as he had done for millions of years. The setting sun had turned crimson and had partly hidden behind Benjora, who appeared sorrowful, the reason for which the young doctor could not fathom. Could he see tears rolling down the old man's face? Tears of sympathy or pity, Raj could not tell for certain. The hapless young man waved to the indigenous elder, expecting Benjora, his only true friend, to wave back. But Benjora stood there, not moving, not smiling, not uttering a word.

"*Veliyelirunna pampine eduthu konathi vechamathiri?* (Have you taken the snake that was happily lying on the fence and put it inside your underwear?)," Benjora seemed to be echoing an old Malayalam proverb.

"Why did you bother to come here?" he asked himself. "You should have stayed in India."

CHAPTER 10

THE FIRST AUTOPSY

Psalm 1
¹ Blessed is the man that walketh not in the
counsel of the ungodly, nor standeth in the way of
sinners, nor sitteth in the seat of the scornful.
² But his delight is in the law of the Lord*; and*
in his law doth he meditate day and night.
³ And he shall be like a tree planted by the rivers of water,
that bringeth forth his fruit in his season; his leaf also
shall not wither; and whatsoever he doeth shall prosper.
⁴ The ungodly are not so: but are like the
chaff which the wind driveth away.
⁵ Therefore the ungodly shall not stand in the judgment,
nor sinners in the congregation of the righteous.
⁶ For the Lord *knoweth the way of the righteous:*
but the way of the ungodly shall perish.

The only matter of interest that happened that week was the autopsy in Derby, an outback port town of about four thousand people on the Broome to Darwin highway and situated about two hundred kilometres from Broome. Jack the autopsy technician, looking very serious, appeared at Raj's office on a Tuesday evening with a request for an autopsy faxed from Derby. An indigenous man of about forty had died of what appeared to be complications of diabetes.

"The hospital will lend us the Toyota Rav 4," he said. "We'll have to leave at seven tomorrow. You can pick it up early in the morning from the hospital garage. Security will help you with that," Jack instructed after handing over the autopsy request.

"I wonder how it will feel driving a Rav 4," Raj mused. "Maybe I shall pick it up tonight and have a whiz around town."

It was not difficult to get the car from the security guys, and Raj went out for a drive that night, taking care not to speed and observing all the road rules. The next morning he picked Jack up from the hospital. He did not appear pleased at all with the Indian doctor.

"Why did you take the car out yesterday?" he shouted. "You were meant to borrow it for today only."

Raj wanted to tell Jack that it was none of his business but decided to be prudent and did not utter a word. "I do not know what is wrong with this fellow; there was nothing wrong in what I did. All I did was drive the car around a bit to get used to it," he thought.

But Raj knew that, strictly speaking, it was wrong to drive the hospital vehicle for nonoffice purposes, and hence he licked his wounds and kept quiet.

Raj noticed that Jack had brought a cardboard packet, about the size of a large dictionary, that he put in the back of the car. They set out at around nine in the morning, with Raj driving and Jack the passenger, but soon their roles were reversed. After about ten minutes, when they hit the highway, Jack started lamenting the difficulties he faced as a passenger.

"I get a migraine and vertigo if I travel in a car that I am not driving," Jack kept complaining.

"Okay, you take over." Raj stopped the car and handed over the wheel to Jack.

From then on for Raj, it was a case of clinging on for dear life. The car took off at 160 kilometres per hour. The road was pretty wide, but still it was a speed that Raj was not accustomed to, except in the movies and during the take-off of aeroplanes. The car sped on at the same speed all the time, without even slowing down at bends and curves.

It was about halfway into the journey that it happened. The car was taking a bend at speed when suddenly a kangaroo streaked across the road, barely a few metres from them, and the car swerved to the right. Before Raj realised it, they had gone off the road at 140 kilometres an hour. The young man felt the pull of the seat belt when the vehicle came to a sudden stop on the sand, still upright, about two hundred metres from the road.

"Oh fuck!" Jack swore and got out.

Raj got out of the car after him. It was a miracle that the car was on its four wheels, and they had avoided serious injury, but the rear door of the soft-roader had opened, and Jack's cardboard packet had been thrown from the car. It was lying about a hundred metres away, with its contents strewn all over the place. Jack ran to the spilt packet, and as Raj started ambling after him, he felt jabbing pain in his left knee. He sat down, clutching it. Raj slowly extended his leg. "No bones broken," he muttered to himself. His knees had hit the glove box during the accident, but the seat belt had protected him from serious injury. The doctor watched the technician, who, unaware of the doctor's suffering, was busy collecting the small bags dispersed across the ground. By the time the pain eased, and Raj slowly got up, Jack had finished picking up the bags and packing them in the cardboard box. As the doctor turned towards the car, he saw one of the bags lying in the bush.

He picked it up; there was a white powdery substance in it, and the young man held it up for a closer inspection.

"Give it to me." Raj looked up to see Jack walking towards him with a snarl on his face.

"He is angry that I didn't help," Raj muttered to himself. "Well...I—" the young doctor's attempted explanation was cut short by the technician, who issued a command.

"Come and give me a push!" he shouted with a scowl. Jack took the bag from the doctor, put it inside the cardboard packet, and deposited it in the back of the car.

The technician got in, started the motor, and shifted to low gear, while Raj put his back to the car and heaved. The car slowly inched towards the road.

Finally, they were back on the highway and travelled the two hundred-odd kilometres to Derby in around one and a half hours. Raj was so concerned about his own survival that he failed to notice the funny-looking boab trees with their bulbous trunks and puny branches shaking in disapproval at their extreme speed.

They reached Derby Hospital at eleven in the morning, the accident delaying them by about half an hour. The pain in Raj's knee had eased completely by now, and he was relieved that there was no serious injury.

The autopsy turned out to be uneventful, until the end.

The deceased was an obese indigenous male, who had died from the complications of diabetes. The treating physician wanted to rule out infection, as infections were common in these circumstances and could contribute to the death of the patient.

In the changing room, Jack and Raj removed their shirts and trousers and slid into green overalls and plastic aprons. Goggles, masks, long rubber gloves, and gumboots completed their attire.

Jack sterilised the blade of a spatula by holding it over a spirit lamp flame and burnt the deceased man's skin over his left nipple. He then passed a sterile syringe with a very long needle to Raj, who punctured the burnt skin and pushed deep to draw blood from the heart, which he transferred into a blood culture bottle. Then, with the deft hands of a well-trained surgeon, he made a long skin incision from under the chin straight down to the diseased man's pubis. Normally mortuary technicians made the skin incisions, but Jack was happy to be a spectator and, like his companion Frank at Royal Kimberley Hospital, always ensured that he did the least physical labour.

"I would have made a Y-shaped incision," commented the wily technician, who was obviously making the point that he was well versed with autopsy techniques. The young doctor did not respond, continuing silently with his dissection; he knew that the Y-shaped incision starting from the end of the collarbones was more popular, but he was more used to making a straight incision from the chin.

Using blunt dissection with the back of his scalpel, Raj peeled the skin away from the deep tissue, as one would open a jacket. The collarbones and the ribs were then cut and separated from their attachment to the breastbone or sternum with the bone scissors. As one would open the front of a shirt, the pathologist opened the chest cavity by pulling the open rib cages to either side.

The lungs were mildly congested but otherwise unremarkable. Raj pulled out the tracheae, or windpipe, and bluntly dissected it and the heart from the posterior or deep part of the chest cavity. With a pair of scissors, the pathologist opened the pulmonary trunk, the main blood vessel that carries blood from the heart to the lungs, and continued opening it past its bifurcation into the right and left pulmonary arteries till they reached the lungs.

"No sign of pulmonary embolism."

Raj's dissection was methodical. He then separated each lung by severing the bronchi, or windpipes, and laid the lungs on the table, where he sliced them as one would slice bread. The lungs appeared soggy and not spongy like normal lungs.

"Terminal lung disease associated with heart failure, nothing dramatic," Raj said to himself.

After he finished the dissection of the lungs, Raj turned his attention to the heart. The coronary vessels, that supply blood to the heart, were markedly narrowed, but this did not surprise the pathologist, as the findings were in keeping with any unfit diabetic. But there was no sign of a heart attack or myocardial infarction.

Raj's attention then turned to the abdominal contents. Before he had started dissecting the lungs and the heart, the young pathologist had separated the gastrointestinal tract and had laid it in a steel basin, expecting the autopsy technician to open and clean the intestines as per the normal custom. But the intestines had not been opened or cleaned, and when he turned around, the doctor saw Jack leaning on the wall, staring at him.

"What about the bowel?" Raj queried, as though it were a normal thing to ask.

"What *about* the bowel?" Jack's reply was a question, his voice slightly raised in a mocking tone.

"I thought you had opened it."

"What are you going to do? Watch me open it?

The doctor did not say anything for some time. "It's okay; I'll open it," he said a minute later and then patiently opened the intestines with a pair of bowel scissors and cleaned them, while Jack watched from a safe distance.

The stomach and the bowel were unremarkable. Raj's attention then turned to the kidneys, which were much smaller than normal and appeared shrunken.

"End-stage kidney disease, an anticipated complication of diabetes; maybe a combination of glomerulosclerosis and pyelonephritis or infection of the kidney," Raj concluded while he weighed the organs and took samples of tissue from each, placing them in jars containing formalin for processing and microscopy. The doctor sat down and quickly dictated the autopsy notes into a Dictaphone before having a shower and changing into his own clothes. When he came out of the changing room, Jack had already sewn the body up, pushed it back into the refrigerator, and disappeared.

Raj waited in the hospital reception for the technician, who returned half an hour later with the car. Before he got in, Raj quickly glanced into the back of the car and was not surprised to see no sign of the cardboard packet.

It was around two thirty in the afternoon when they started the return journey to Broome. Raj did not even attempt to drive, as he had on the onward journey; Jack drove at his breakneck speed, and by four they were back at the hospital.

"It's better you return the car, since you signed it out. You've to sign the car back in," Jack said, handing the keys back before getting out.

Raj took the keys from Jack hesitantly, walked around to the driver's seat, got in, and drove to the garage. Before leaving the garage, the doctor opened the back door to the luggage space and had a quick look around. There was a white envelope lying there. Raj took the envelope and found that there was no address written on it and that it was not sealed. He opened it and took out a slip of paper, on which there was a message scribbled. It began with "Dear RR" and was signed "SS."

"Sending you the stuff as promised. See you soon," it said.

The young man slid the letter back into the envelope and put the envelope into his pocket before walking to the security office and signing the register.

"How did the autopsy go?" Dr. Stich enquired on Raj's return to the office. The elderly pathologist was standing near Sarah's desk, chatting with her.

"Nothing unusual—an indigenous man with end-stage kidney disease and probable infection. I didn't get any help from Jack to open the bowel."

"Yeah, don't ever expect any help from him."

"I wanted to put my foot down and make him do it."

"I won't say that's wise; those guys are extremely crafty. I won't fight them; they know they can get you."

"There is something else I wanted to tell you," Raj said after some hesitation.

"Well, come in." Dr. Stich motioned Raj towards his office, and Raj followed him.

Raj then told him about the accident, how Jack's packet was thrown off the car and about the bags containing the white powder.

"I am just worried what the white powder is," Raj muttered.

"What do you think it is? Did you think it was heroin?" Dr. Stich said as though reading Raj's thoughts.

"I was just wondering."

The answer to this was loud laughter from the elderly pathologist. "Ha-ha!" He laughed for almost a minute. "However evil and clever he is, I do not think he is capable of trafficking."

"I couldn't help him to retrieve the bags, because I had a knee injury, nothing serious, but it appeared he did not like my handling those bags," Raj said.

"That is his nature. Don't you worry about that."

The young man got up from the chair. "I thought I should mention this to you." He then got out of the room and started walking towards his office, his head down, deep in thought. Raj did not tell his boss about Jack's brief vanishing act after finishing the autopsy, the disappearance of the packet from the car, or the envelope that he found in the car.

"I do not understand," he thought. "Not capable of trafficking? What does that mean?"

The young doctor left his office a little earlier than usual, as he was tired by the day's events, and as he walked home that evening, his shoulders were hunched and his head bent. As if by second nature, the young man searched the horizon for his friend Benjora. The sun was directly above Benjora's head, and the glare was so strong that Raj had to look away. "Be of courage," Raj's mother seemed to tell him. He could hear her words from afar, reading to him the first psalm, "Blessed is the man that walketh not in the counsel of the ungodly..."

Raj straightened and lifted his chin. His walk became steadier and more purposeful, and he started humming an old Malayalam love song.

CHAPTER 11

JAUNDICE

Moottath´e moollekku manamilla.
("The Jasmine in your own garden
does not have any scent.")

Even in this weird place, there were some specks of goodness. Raj had a lot of affection and respect for Maria, the Eritrean scientist, while the other person who commanded his love and respect was Sarah, the secretary.

Sometimes during the tea breaks, Sarah and Raj would go out for a cuppa, when they would have a chat. Occasionally David, the chief scientist, joined them. The hospital café was a busy place, where many of the nursing staff came for refreshments, as did the patients. A large number of the patients were Aboriginal people, who looked very unwell. Their faces were swollen due to kidney failure caused by diabetes; white nurses pushed them around in wheelchairs. There were, in addition, many inmates from the mental health ward, most of who were not psychiatric patients but drug addicts and petrol sniffers.

Many petrol sniffers also hung around in the city next to the bus stands and markets. Raj would gaze at them with sympathy, these scrawny unkempt teenagers in rags with matted hair and beards clinging to old empty plastic cans that they would bring to their noses periodically. Their faces would then light up as they greedily sniffed the bottle for the whiff of life-giving petrol. These cans were prized possessions, and when one of them sniffed, the others would gaze at the can longingly for their turn. Raj felt extremely unhappy and sorry for these pathetic examples of humankind.

"There, but for the grace of God, goes Raj," Raj thought, quoting one of his father's favourite sayings, and thanked his Creator.

"Why are you looking at them?" Sarah asked.

"I do not know why. I was wondering why humankind should exist in many different states. There are scientists who would spend their lives trying to figure out how to inhabit Mars, and then there are places where people spend hours trying to make and improve bombs to destroy civilisation. Then there are people like this who have descended to a life lower than that of animals. Why is Africa worse off free? Nobody in Africa died of hunger when Africa was under white rule. With self-rule, there is not only hunger but also death, fire, and famine as well as loss of freedom. Why do dynasties rule India? Why has democracy in India deteriorated into reigns by elected kings and queens? Why do so many people have to die on the roads in India each year, a number that is more than the population of many small countries?"

"Well, many people die of shooting in the United States," Sarah said. "The argument is that if everybody has guns, nobody will dare to shoot at anybody for fear of being shot at."

"Then why should they worry if Iran has nuclear weapons? The United States should be supplying every country in the world with nuclear weapons to avoid a nuclear war," Raj countered. Raj and Sarah knew these arguments and banter would get them nowhere, but they liked to talk such nonsense sometimes.

Although Raj believed Sarah was perfect, or near perfect, Dr. Stich would sometimes get angry with her. That morning Raj had heard him shouting at her from his office.

"I thought I heard the boss upset today," he said as Sarah picked up her bag and prepared to leave.

"Oh no, that was nothing. He wanted something included in the report, and I forgot to type it."

"*Moottath'e moollekku manamilla*," Raj murmured something in Malayalam.

"What did you say?"

"The jasmine in your own garden does not have any scent. Well, it means that Dr. Stich is so used to having you around that he does not realise, or he has forgotten, how good you are."

Sarah got up. "Thanks for your kind words." She smiled. "I'm leaving now," she said and started walking towards the car park. Though her boss would sometimes give her a hard time, Sarah felt happy with life. Her husband had been promoted to the supervisor of the workshop where he worked, her son was the vice-captain of the school footy team, and her daughter was turning into a tall and pretty woman with model-like features and was on her way to becoming a professional ballet dancer. Sarah found the new pathology registrar funny. True, it took her a while to get used to his accent, but she found his English to be surprisingly good, even if at times he faltered.

Sarah was an exceptional secretary. Raj could dictate almost anything on the Dictaphone, but when Sarah typed it, she adjusted the minor grammar mistakes, and the reports came out perfectly.

She had walked a few steps when she stopped and walked back.

"I noticed something with your eyes." She walked a bit closer to Raj.

"What about my eyes?"

"They are a bit yellow."

"Maybe it is the dust."

"Maybe."

Sarah did not linger anymore.

It was five in the evening, and since he had finished the day's work, Raj did not stay any longer either. He walked home and, on entering the unit, glanced in the mirror. Yes, his eyes were mildly yellow; there was no doubt about that.

That night Raj had stomach pain so severe that he doubled up with the pain and could not sleep at all. The young doctor did not have any painkillers except Panadol. He tried a couple of them, but to no avail. Luckily by morning, the pain had abated, and since it was a Saturday, Raj slept the entire day.

CHAPTER 12

JOHN LARGEBONE

"His name is John Largebone," Dr. Stich announced one morning. "He is an English pathologist trained in the UK. He is joining us as a consultant."

Dr. Largebone's arrival, though expected, was very sudden. It happened just a week after Dr. Stich revealed the news to his staff. The morning that he arrived, John seemed to appear out of nowhere, sitting ramrod straight like an apparition in the office that Iqbaal had used. The English pathologist did not introduce himself, nor did Dr. Stich bother to introduce him to Raj.

Raj decided to introduce himself.

"Hi there, I'm Raj." He had borrowed Dr. Stich's policy of standing at the doorway. It looked as though John was fiddling with his microscope; maybe he was cleaning it. He slowly turned towards Raj, but there was no smile on his face, nor was there enmity. Dr. Largebone's deep-blue eyes betrayed no emotions, his expression vacant. His eyes looked as though they were gazing at the horizon. John's appearance was impeccable, his shirt and trousers ironed smoothly without a single crease, and his short blond hair was neatly parted.

The English doctor got up from his chair and moved towards Raj in a slow, fluid motion. He extended his hand. Raj shook it as if by reflex; John's grip was firm, but his eyes were still fixed on the horizon.

"Nice to meet you," he said. "I remember Dr. Stich mentioning your name." The clipped accent did not make the low monotonous speech enjoyable to listen to, and the pleasantries ended as abruptly as they had started, as the English doctor turned and walked back to his chair. Raj knew that the meeting had ended, and he returned to his office.

John's surname—Largebone—certainly was exactly opposite to his physique, as he was extremely thin and looked like a reed. He always walked straight without looking to either side, and as he walked, he appeared to float. The English doctor had a long, thin European nose, a mildly receding chin, and short hair that he kept oiled and parted even while he slept. John always wore formal shirts and trousers; jeans and shorts were not part of his wardrobe, even in the hot and humid Broome summer. The sight of the English doctor gave Raj such an eerie feeling that he was sure John was a ghost or even a corpse breathed into life by Lucifer himself.

Raj particularly tried to avoid seeing John at night.

Dr. Largebone paid Raj scant attention. The Englishman's knowledge of pathology was so vast and deep that he lived, breathed, and talked the subject. During his brief conversations with John, Raj found that he knew the names of the inventors of the fluorescent microscope, the electron microscope, and the dark-field microscope. The English pathologist knew how to convert an ordinary microscope into a dark-field microscope. John was well versed with who first described adult T-cell lymphoma leukaemia and who first described phaeochromocytoma. Dr. Largebone, it seemed, had no other life but pathology, and doing autopsies appeared to be what he loved the most. He could talk for hours on various autopsy techniques. John knew how to get to the head of the thigh bone, or femur, from the anterior and posterior aspects, and he could expose the spinal cord from the front and back too.

John lived alone and appeared indifferent to the fairer sex. For him, they were not interesting, and he believed his life was better spent in pursuing the study of pathology: the science of disease.

"Maybe the part of the body that gives people the ability to love or lust is poorly developed in John," Raj thought.

In addition to being an exceptional pathologist, Dr. Largebone was also good at making gadgets. Some of his gadgets were quite innovative—for example, the tissue gadget. The toilet tissue in the public toilet was always kept locked with only the tongue of the roll sticking out. John would attach his machine under the toilet roll and would feed the tongue of the tissue paper onto the roller on his gadget. The machine had a motor, and it would roll the tissue paper onto itself.

Raj soon noticed Sarah the secretary complaining about John's fast depletion of the batteries used in his Dictaphone. Raj knew that Dr. Largebone was using those batteries to run his tissue gadget.

Dr. Stich took to John. He liked John's knowledge and enthusiasm, and this newfound love increased his loathing for Raj.

"Autopsies are his forte," Sarah commented a week after the arrival of the English pathologist.

Dr. Largebone certainly had extensive experience conducting autopsies. Raj had a quick search on the Internet and found out that John had authored several articles based on various autopsies that he had performed in the United Kingdom. Most of these were interesting case reports, where unexpected findings turned up, but there were also some case series, including one on botulism toxicity–associated deaths in the elderly.

The English pathologist was multitalented, and his contract allowed him to do extra duties in the hospital. In addition to his registration as a histopathologist, Dr. Largebone also had forensic pathology registration and general medical registration. As a result, he did medico-legal autopsies when the resident forensic pathologist was out of town and also worked as a resident medical officer one day a week. It seemed the English doctor liked to look after his patients in life and in death.

Even before coming to Australia, Dr. Largebone used to perform forensic autopsies in addition to medical autopsies, and he related some of his experiences as a forensic pathologist to Raj. Once, when he was working in the United Kingdom, John was called to perform an autopsy on an unusual death at a farm. As he investigated his cases thoroughly, he went to the farm to examine the scene of death firsthand.

The story goes like this. A middle-aged farmer had been found dead one morning, under a cow. This man was using the cow for his nocturnal adventures, but that fateful night, the angel of death awaited him instead of perverted pleasure. The cow kicked him in his head, and he fell down unconscious. The animal then lay on top of him and had a nap, while the unfortunate farmer died of asphyxiation. On examination, the dead man had concussion, his penis was covered with mucus and cow dung, and his lungs showed marked congestion, oedema, and haemorrhage.

"It is safer to be a shepherd than a cattleman," John said, and Raj readily agreed.

CHAPTER 13

THE VIETNAMESE TIME BOMB

John's penchant for autopsies was rewarded about a week after his joining the department.

"I have an autopsy," Dr. Largebone announced that Monday morning, sounding very enthusiastic. Raj was not particularly fond of autopsies—he certainly did not wait in eagerness for them to arrive—but he did not detest them either. The Indian pathologist was barely in his office after the weekend and had not yet settled in when John arrived with the patient's notes.

"May I come along?" Raj enquired. Raj was always happy to extract some extra knowledge without resorting to spending hours on books, and the English doctor was more than willing to teach him.

The two mortuary technicians were waiting for the pathologists, as was the body, which was already undressed and laid out on the autopsy table.

Paul Winter, an American soldier on leave, had died of cancer of the kidney, which in medical terms was known as renal cell carcinoma. He was on a tour around the world, had finished the Asian leg of his tour, and was in Australia when he suddenly became sick. He was admitted to Royal Kimberley Hospital a week before he died. A CT scan had revealed a kidney tumour with secondary spread to the lungs and liver. Raj carefully read his notes before the autopsy started.

"There's something fishy here," John announced, pointing to the patient's temperature chart. His temperature had hovered above 40 degrees Celsius the whole week that Paul was ill.

"Though fever is a common presenting feature in cancer of the kidney, it's not usually of such high grade in renal cancers. Paul died within a week of contracting the fever, which is also unusual for cancer of the kidney. Let's look at the blood-culture report." John's voice drawled with its usual lack of emotion.

"No pathogenic bacteria grown. Mixed organisms, including Staphylococcus and Pseudomonas—contaminants," the report said.

The treating clinicians had debated on performing a fine needle aspiration of the kidney tumour but had finally decided against it, as kidney tumours were sometimes known to spread along the needle track. Further, Paul's condition deteriorated fast, and he died before any invasive investigation could be done.

Fine-needle biopsies involve putting ordinary injection needles into a tumour and examining the material under the microscope. The procedure obviates the need for an open biopsy with a knife and is hence safe to perform in very ill patients.

Paul was certainly good looking and looked very much like an American soldier. His blue eyes stared at the ceiling, his blond hair was cut close to the scalp, and his nose was thin and long. Lean but powerfully muscled, Paul could have been a triathlonist.

The pathologists soon changed into green overalls, plastic aprons, and the rest of their lab attire. As they always do before they cut open the body, Dr. Largebone sterilised, with a red-hot spatula, the skin on the right side of the left nipple and drew blood from the heart of the deceased for culture. He then started making incisions while the mortuary technicians and Raj watched.

The chest, or pleural cavity, was filled with blood, and the lungs looked congested or reddish from the outside.

John then separated each lung by severing the bronchi and laid them on the table where he sliced them like bread slices. The lungs had not collapsed, as a normal lung would after death, but were soggy and filled with fluid and hence easy to cut. There were multiple cavities filled with brownish pus in both lungs.

"Abscess," the English pathologist muttered without looking up.

"I agree. I cannot see any tumour," Raj commented. The English doctor did not respond. His whole concentration was on the autopsy as he put one-centimetre cubed pieces of the necrotic areas into sterile culture bottles.

Paul's heart was fine: the coronary arteries—the blood vessels supplying the heart muscle—did not even have an iota of fat, and, as expected in a young and fit person, they were as clean as a whistle. The heart valves also appeared normal.

Upon finishing the dissection of the chest contents, the doctors turned their attention to the abdominal cavity. They quickly opened the intestines and cleaned them. The mortuary technicians did not help with opening the intestines, content to be spectators as usual, but John was so engrossed with the autopsy that he did not even notice that the bowels were not opened and cleaned by the technicians, as is the normal custom elsewhere.

On examination, the stomach and the bowel were unremarkable.

The attention of the two doctors then turned to the kidneys, liver, and spleen. Most of the left kidney had been replaced by a cavity filled with pus, while there were multiple smaller cavities in the right kidney and also in the liver and the spleen.

"Necrotic renal cell carcinoma with multiple secondaries? Or is it something else?" Dr. Largebone mused.

"It looks odd for cancer. I cannot see a mass," Raj agreed. "But we have to wait for the microscopy."

The Dead Shall Teach The Living

Cancers can be necrotic and can present as cavitating tumours that can be mistaken for abscesses, but even in these cases, the tumours would be part cavity and part solid tumour. That was not the case here, with all lesions consisting of cavities filled with pus and having no solid tumour component.

The pathologists put multiple pieces of tissue from the lungs, liver, kidney, and spleen into jars containing formalin for further histopathology processing. They made some smears by touching the raw tissue onto the glass slides.

Two days later the slides were ready.

"Shall we look at the slides together?" said the English doctor, inviting Raj to view the slides with him on a multiheaded microscope. Though John's social life was almost nonexistent, and he was a recluse, when it came to pathology, he was enthusiastic and liked to include others in his search for truth. They sat at a multiheaded microscope and peered at the slides. None of the sections revealed any tumour; instead, there were abscesses or cavities filled with pus and granulomas or collections of inflammatory cells called macrophages.

"We'll do some stains for fungi and tuberculosis," Raj said, as these were the organisms that usually produced granulomas in the tissue they infected.

They went back to their respective offices and were soon engrossed in their routine work.

After about two hours, there was a knock on the door.

"Here you are. The stains are ready." Maria's smile was infectious. Raj marvelled at her beauty and poise. She was wearing a black T-shirt and white skirt that reached just above her knees and hugged her buttocks. Raj caught a glimpse of her firm breasts as she put the slides on the desk, and the girl, sensing his gaze, smiled mischievously and turned away.

"No fungi, no tuberculosis. We will do some stains for atypical mycobacteria," Dr. Largebone said. Atypical mycobacteria are bacteria related to tuberculosis bacteria, but they produce infections in people whose natural defences or immunity are suppressed as in AIDS patients or patients on anticancer drugs.

Again Maria was prompt with her work and was back with the slides within the hour.

"No bacteria seen," John concluded after peering at the slides for half an hour. "We will wait for the culture report."

The English pathologist dialled the chief microbiology scientist. Being a small lab, they did not have an infectious-disease specialist or a medical microbiologist on board all the time. The microbiology lab was managed by scientists who were not keen to take orders from histopathologists.

Anne, the chief microbiology scientist, was a very stern lady of about fifty years of age.

"Hello." She was polite but brusque.

"Hi, this is John here from histo. We have a peculiar case." He then proceeded to tell her about it—how Paul was travelling around the world when he contracted high-grade fever after visiting the Far East.

"I feel this is some kind of weird organism. We would like the culture to be followed up until all the organisms are speciated, even if they appear to be contaminants." Dr. Largebone was crisp and clear.

"We will do exactly as you tell us." Anne was stern, but she understood medicine better than many doctors and realised straightaway what John was trying to tell her.

A week on and Raj had forgotten about the case. He was in his office at work, peering down the microscope, when Dr. Largebone paused at his office and put a slip of paper onto his desk.

"What did I tell you?" John's query was more like a statement.

Raj took a quick look at the culture report and saw "Burkholderia pseudomallei grown."

"Melioidosis," the English pathologist continued. "I knew it would be this." His voice betrayed no passion or jubilation, even though the discovery was sensational. His countenance was still that of a champion poker player.

"We have an appointment with the infectious-disease specialist next week," John announced before returning to his office.

The infectious-disease specialist, Susan Stuyvesant, came to Royal Kimberley Hospital only once a fortnight for a couple of days when she flew in from Perth to look at important cases. Sometimes she wouldn't visit for a few months; other times she would stay for a month at one stretch.

She had extensive knowledge of her subject. She had led a remarkable number of studies and authored several articles in peer-reviewed journals. Most of these studies involved a lot of physical labour, for which Susan found a solution by employing workers from the third world. Dr. Stuyvesant arranged for scholarships for microbiologists from the developing world to do clinical attachments in Australia. These scholarships were just enough for the sustenance of these enthusiastic young doctors who thought it a great honour to work with a distinguished microbiologist in Australia. Thus, Susan always had a team of Indians, Pakistanis, and Africans working on her various projects for measly wages, much below the minimum legal wage for an Australian. They toiled for a scrap of paper called a certificate that they would get at the end of their six months or one year. Sometimes their names would appear in a journal as the fourth or fifth author of an article. It was modern-day slavery by mutual consent.

The pathologists were escorted to Dr. Susan Stuyvesant's office by her secretary the next Monday morning. Raj had seen Dr. Stuyvesant once before at a meeting. She was an imposing lady. In her heyday she may well have been pretty, and even now, though jaded looking and overweight, she carried herself with the dignity of an old racehorse. Susan's fifty years showed in her girth, which she had accumulated mainly below her waist. Her upper torso was relatively thin compared to her massive rump and thighs, which could easily knock down a sumo wrestler.

Raj thought she resembled a huge cone-shaped caramel pudding that had been taken out of the fridge and left at room temperature for a short time and had collapsed in on itself, creating a massive bottom compared with a smaller, but still substantial, upper portion.

The Indian pathologist could not help smiling when he recalled James the lab manager's words. "Dr. Stich has been courting Susan for a long time, but she has not returned his affection. In fact, she hates him so much that she would kill him if he pressed on with his advances. I know how she would kill him; she would sit on his face, and he would slowly suffocate. Dr. Stich would be found dead with a smile on his face—dead but happy in his final minutes." James always emphasised the word "doctor" when he used it to refer to the famous pathologist.

"How are you?" Raj was woken from his musing by the smiling double chin and the large extended hand of the microbiologist. Her handshake was cheerful and hearty and moderately painful. Seeing the grimace on Raj's face, Dr. Largebone sat down and started fiddling through a journal as though trying to find a certain page. Susan stared at the English pathologist for a moment, gave up the idea of the welcoming handshake, and sat down heavily in her chair.

"This is John…" Before Raj could finish the introduction, Susan had rudely interrupted him and had started talking.

"Excellent, really excellent. We thought these diseases were a thing of the past. Surely the ghosts of the dead Vietnamese still haunt the Americans, especially the American soldiers." Susan Stuyvesant's voice was slow and punctuated but accurate and clear like a cold knife pressed to your heart on a dark night. She paused after each word and carefully selected her next word. She slowly explained how many cases of melioidosis had occurred in Australia within the past ten years. One could contract the terrible disease in tropical Northern Australia or in the tropical Far East, particularly Vietnam, where it was more common and endemic. Susan then passed Raj the textbook of infectious diseases, with a page indicated by a bookmark. Raj took the page and read.

"Melioidosis, also known as the 'Vietnamese time bomb' is an infection American soldiers used to contract during the Vietnam War. The disease is caused by bacteria called Burkholderia pseudomallei found in the tropical soil from where it enters the body through abrasions. The infections have a long incubation period, during which time the person is apparently well, and will manifest usually months or years after exposure when it presents with acute and devastating effect. Unless diagnosed promptly and treated with a mixture of very potent antibiotics, the disease is usually fatal. The causative bacteria of melioidosis is a dangerous organism to work with in the lab, though human-to-human transmission has not been reported."

John sat there as though uninterested all through this discourse. Of course, he knew much more about melioidosis than either of them.

Half an hour later, on the way out, Raj discovered that Dr. Largebone knew a lot more about the famous microbiologist than most people in Broome.

"She is a lesbian," John said in his usual monotonous drone.

"Who?"

"Dr. Stuyvesant. Her lover is one of her scientists. Her name is Jane Barlett. Jane also acts as her spy and does dirty work for her like dobbing on the staff." Dr. Largebone continued his soliloquy without stopping and without glancing at the Indian pathologist.

Raj was amazed at the English pathologist's general knowledge, and though he was confident that the English doctor was telling the truth, he did not bother to ask him how he acquired this piece of sensitive news.

"Unusual tropical disease revisited" was the title of the case report that came out in the *Journal of Tropical Pathology* a few months later. The article was authored by Dr. John Largebone of Royal Kimberley Hospital and co-authored by Dr. Susan Stuyvesant.

A week later Raj did not fail to notice the headline on the second page of the *Broome Herald,* the local newspaper: "Parents of deceased American soldier in Broome." Normally Raj would have disregarded such news, but this time he bought the paper and read it thoroughly. Paul Winter's parents had written to the health minister that their son's treatment was inadequate and that it had contributed to his death. They were now in Broome to expedite the inquiry.

Raj told John about his stomach pain and yellow eyes, or jaundice, not because the English doctor was a friend but because he seemed to know everything about diseases. He seemed very concerned and asked Raj a lot of questions. How did the pain begin? Was it slow in onset? Was it associated with alcohol? And all the usual questions a doctor would ask a jaundiced patient.

CHAPTER 14

DR. STICH AND BALD NUNS

"DIRECTOR OF HISTOPATHOLOGY" read the sign in front of Dr. Stich's office. Even though Dr. Stich was the director, he had little control over the six histopathology staff members.

Raj's thoughts wandered to Kuttan and Kuttan's restaurant back home in Calicut—or Kozhikode, as it is now called—in his beautiful Kerala in South India. Kuttan was the proprietor and director of Kuttan's restaurant. "Kuttan's and Kuttan" was the nickname the medics gave to the small teashop and its owner near their hostel in Calicut, the city where Raj studied medicine.

During their medical-school days, the medics would stroll from their hostel to the small teashop for a cuppa or snack to break the monotony of the backbreaking long hours of study. They wore their beautiful multicoloured loincloth, or lungi, "without"—that is, without underwear—their balls hanging down, thanks to the warm weather, where they swung like pendulums and hit their thighs rhythmically as they walked, clang...clang.

Kuttan, the restaurant proprietor, was middle aged and of medium build. He never wore a shirt. He would sit behind his desk in his lungi, his hair drenched in oil, which seeped down his damp face. The mixture of oil and sweat gave the man a unique damp, sweet odour. He always had stubble; hair grew on his ears, and matted hair spilt from under his arms like ferns from a crevice. Kuttan constantly chewed tobacco with betel leaves, the red juice of which he spat every now and then through the gap between his front teeth.

Raj and his friends would enter the shop and place their order. Kuttan would shout the order to his cook in the kitchen behind. The medics would go to their table and wait for the meal to arrive. Kuttan would then disappear from his perch behind the desk. One day, ever curious, Raj peeped into the kitchen where he could see Kuttan cooking the dish. After a while, Kuttan would be back behind his desk and would shout to his waiter to bring the food. Again, Kuttan would disappear, only to reappear in the role of the waiter with the food, which he then served. The same ritual followed for table cleaning. Finally, the customers paid Kuttan the money. For Kuttan, he was the proprietor and director of his shop with many workers under him, and that thought gave him a lot of comfort.

After their cuppa, the medics would walk back to the hostel, clang...clang.

Dr. Stich also brought back other memories, memories of Raj's childhood laced with tears and nightmares. The elderly pathologist had started finding mistakes in every report that Raj wrote and every slide he examined and would often come to Raj's office asking him why the work was not ready. Dr. Stich did not waste any opportunity to belittle Raj: his reports, his English, his grammar, his pronunciation, and even his manners were wrong. The elderly pathologist's feelings for India also changed from love to intense hatred, reflecting his newfound loathing for the young doctor from the subcontinent.

For Raj, any questioning was out of the question, as this would mean the loss of his job and good-bye to his dream of acquiring a Western degree.

As Raj watched, the elderly pathologist's face changed slowly, his grey hair transforming into a white hood and his aged face losing its wrinkles and becoming the sweet and innocent face of a woman in her early twenties. Dr. Stich's enormous bulk slowly reduced in front of Raj's eyes, and he metamorphosised into Sister Angelica, the beautiful nun at Raj's primary school. Almost all the nuns in Kerala in those days had shaved heads hidden under white hoods and were known as "baldies" among the hapless students they taught. Raj and his friends always wondered about the stubble on their shaven heads under their hoods.

Sister Veronica, the headmistress at Sacred Heart School, gave the sweetest smile on her wrinkled face when Raj's dad brought Raj in for registration.

But the three years that Raj spent there were a long nightmare.

No talking, no running, no games, and no laughter was the motto of the school. Entire lessons had to be learnt by rote, and the silliest spelling mistakes were treated with a caning. The canes were almost three to four feet long, and they were used regularly—sometimes on outstretched hands, sometimes the legs, and often the buttocks. Girls were beaten less often than boys, but when that happened, the boys derived some sadistic pleasure as their knee-length skirts curled over the cane, exposing their lovely brown thighs for the briefest second.

Sister Angelica, the mathematics teacher, was particularly cruel, and often the children punted as to who would be the lucky one not to be whipped that day.

Sister Angelica's father, Pathrose, was a liquor baron. His very popular concoctions were made with cheap spirits, making him extremely rich. Pathrose paid a hefty sum regularly to all the political parties to keep off the long arm of the law, he made large offerings to the church, and he promised his firstborn to the good Lord as a return for business success. Pathrose's first child, Santhi, was a beautiful and very bright girl, who, in addition, was a natural leader and a good student. She was brilliant in her studies and flourished in extracurricular activities. The only blotch to her innocent early life was that in her high-school days, she fell in love with a handsome young boy. She would have married him, but for her father's promise to the Lord.

Her father beckoned her to him one day soon after her eighteenth birthday.

"Santhi," he said. "I have something very important to tell you. I have promised the Lord that you will be His bride."

Santhi went into a swoon. All her dreams were shattered, but like most good Catholic girls, she obeyed her father, and the young lady became Sister Angelica, the Lord's bride. Instead of life as a university student, her life became confined within the cold walls of the convent, and to break the monotony, the young nun accepted the teacher's job at Sacred Heart English Medium School at Alwaye, Raj's hometown.

That particular day the history teacher had not arrived, and the children started chatting with gusto. Suddenly there was a flurry of steps led by a long cane held by a hand in long white sleeves. The cane landed on the chests of the children and across their backs. When the din abated slightly, Raj looked back, like a reflex.

"How dare you look back?" With rapid strides, Sister Angelica pounced on the hapless boy, and the cane moved swiftly and remorselessly, with Raj's body burning and writhing with each lash.

Within a few minutes, Sister Angelica had finished her punishment and made a rapid exit, striding towards the convent as if on a mission. Even though his flesh still stung from the whipping, Raj leapt from his chair and stealthily followed the nun, who passed through the gate between the school and a semipartitioned courtyard. The boy followed his teacher at a safe distance into the courtyard, and for a moment he stood overwhelmed by the beauty he saw.

This place looked different from all the places he had ever been before. Raj was transfixed by a most beautiful sight, an impossibly green garden where marigolds, jacarandas, chrysan-themums, dahlias, and jasmine vines grew intermingled with each other. Butterflies and dragonflies floated around the garden. In the middle of the garden stood a chapel covered with ivy. Peace and calmness lingered in the air. Sister Angelica's pace softened, and the anger on her face changed to grief. The chapel did not have any doors, and as the young nun entered the building, Raj followed her up to the entrance, where he paused. Though it was a catholic chapel, there were no idols or statues, but behind the altar was a French window, looking through which the boy was astonished to see a gorgeous rippling stream.

The nun was kneeling before the altar, and Raj could hear her sobbing. After a short while, Sister Angelica got up and walked slowly out of the church and out of the garden. Raj moved into the bushes, out of sight, while the young woman passed by.

The boy then entered the chapel and kneeled down before the altar. He closed his eyes and started praying. As any boy brought up in a Christian family, Raj prayed for himself, his parents, and siblings. In his little innocent heart, he begged for himself and his friends to be saved from the daily whipping. He paused a short while before continuing.

"Forgive the teachers who whip me, because they do not know that they are harming us. Forgive Sister Angelica." In his prayer, the boy passed through the window behind the altar and stepped into the stream, before immersing himself in its cooling water. When he came out of the stream, the boy became aware of a man with a calm face standing nearby. As Raj looked at the man, he walked over, bent and picked him up, and held him close to his chest. Raj clung to him and sobbed.

When Raj opened his eyes after the prayer, the man and the stream had disappeared. He got up, and peace and calmness came over him as he walked back to class.

CHAPTER 15

RIDES AT THE BROOME SHOW,
AUTO-RICKSHAWS AND BUS RIDES IN INDIA

With Vidya being away, Raj experienced severe loneliness and boredom. To while away the time that Saturday, the young pathologist went to the Broome Royal Show.

He went by himself, since he particularly abhorred company on such occasions. There were farm animals and equipment on show as well as various rides. The young doctor wandered through the farm exhibits and came to the rides area, where he tried a few. On one of the rides, Raj had to sit in a small cage that was attached to two giant pillars about fifty metres high with huge elastic bands. The cage was catapulted into the sky but straightaway sprang back to earth, pulled by the elastic bands. Raj's chair spun within the cage as it yo-yoed, but he thought the ride was funny, not inspiring or scary. Next, the young Indian doctor rode on a giant merry-go-round, which spun in every conceivable direction. Some of his fellow riders went into hysterics, and one fainted. Even here Raj found the ride funny but far from scary.

Raj was thoroughly bored. These rides were definitely dull after rides in the auto-rickshaws in India, the tiny three-wheeled scooter taxis known by their pet name, "auto." They were part of the landscape of any town in his home country, where they provided cheap transport for the public. The driver would sit in the front, the vehicle carrying two to five passengers, two on either side of him and three in the seat behind, comfortably or crowded as the case may be. The autos have no seat belts or doors. The passenger hops into the back seat, and before your bum is in, the vehicle takes off with such acceleration that you are thrown to the back of the seat. You pull yourself in just in time to see an enormous truck coming straight at you. At the last second the auto veers off with a hairbreadth between the two vehicles. After a few moments, before you dare to breathe, the auto takes a U-turn and joins the rushing traffic in the opposite direction. Then you suddenly see a transport bus looming on your right and edging your auto into the enormous pothole on the roadside. The bus conductor is hanging out of the bus, holding onto the rails at the door of the bus and shouting obscenities at the auto driver. The auto jumps out of the pothole just in time to escape a rushing water buffalo that has decided that the auto is a cow buffalo in heat. You cling to the bar that separates the passenger compartment from the driver's seat. If you are a novice, you will shut your eyes and bite on the driver's seat in front to avoid screaming. Whether novice or experienced, the thrill and the adrenaline rush you get from these adventures never reduce in intensity. The excitement of the adventure only increases when the next day's newspaper announces in its middle pages that eight people died on the roads in Ernakulam city that day.

These road trips, in addition to giving the passengers the extreme thrill of brushing with instant death, also dealt raw humour, sometimes, adding stale spice to their otherwise boring routine. Raj recalled one such incident that happened when he was going to school one day.

The private operators, in an attempt to get the largest number of commuters, raced their buses with each other. These buses never stopped but only slowed down at bus stops, which meant that the passengers had to either jump out or jump onto the moving bus. The bus conductor would assist by either pushing them out or pulling them in. That day the bus conductor used slightly more force than usual as he pushed an old man out of the bus onto the roadside. The octogenarian fell down, but to everybody's surprise, he got up quickly and showed his indignation by lifting his white loincloth, or *mundu,* and exposing himself to the conductor, a sight shared by the other passengers. The conductor wanted to react to this extreme act of obscenity, but he found it hard to return it in kind, as he was wearing trousers, and the bus was already gathering speed. So he lifted the loincloth of a passenger who was standing next to him. For some reason, the passengers did not share with the conductor this doctrine of retribution, so they manhandled him. They pushed him out of the bus, jumped on top of him, and gave him such a hiding that he limped for the rest of his life.

CHAPTER 16

JOHN'S MEETING ON AUTOPSIES

"We should be doing more autopsies," Dr. Largebone announced one morning. Raj had finished the day's cut-up, taking bits from specimens for processing, and was in his office checking the slides under the microscope when John peeped into Raj's office to make this statement.

"I think we're doing enough," Raj responded. He clearly enjoyed life more than death.

"No, we are not. You know about the soldier's autopsy. I'd met with the clinicians and insisted on the autopsy. I'd a feeling that the diagnosis was wrong."

"How did you know about this patient?"

"I'd seen him during one of my ward duties, and his case was presented in one of the clinical meetings before the patient died. I attend most clinical meetings."

"I'm happy with the number of autopsies that I'm doing." Raj expressed his distaste for cutting open dead bodies. "Anyway, what are you going to do to increase the number of autopsies?"

"Well, you don't have to do the autopsies. I'll do them myself. If you're interested, you can come and watch, and maybe lend me a hand. I'm going to have a meeting with the clinicians, especially the unit heads, to try to persuade them to ask us for more autopsies. Although I work in the wards once a week, I can't request the next of kin for autopsies, as only the department heads have that privilege."

There has been a marked reduction in the number of medical autopsies all over the world in recent years compared to the olden days when all or most hospital deaths were autopsied. There are three main reasons for this decline in number. First, with all the modern investigative techniques, the clinicians believe that they have the correct diagnosis and do not believe that autopsies are required. Secondly, with the public becoming very litigious, the doctors do not want to be confronted with any new findings that may not corroborate the antemortem diagnosis. Thirdly, with reports of organs from dead bodies being used for teaching and exhibitions in museums, the relatives are increasingly reluctant to give permission for autopsies.

John's meeting with the clinicians about autopsies took place the next week. Although he did not quite like the agenda, Raj attended the meeting. Dr. Largebone was energetic, and his organisational skills were evident that day, as at least twenty clinicians, including heads of departments, attended the function.

"Autopsies were the main method of studying medicine in the near past," the English pathologist began. "Nowadays, with the advent of noninvasive and invasive procedures, which can give us most of the diagnosis before the patient's death, we tend not to ask for autopsies. This, coupled with the issue of organ misuse for museum exhibitions and studies, without the proper consent of the relatives, has made many of us wary of requesting autopsies. However, I can assure you we can still learn a lot from autopsies. We can confirm the diagnosis. In a few cases, we may learn that we pursued a wrong diagnosis. Moreover, we will come across a lot of things that could have contributed to the patient's death that we may have never thought of. I give you my word that the organs will be properly treated as per the organ-retention laws." John, who, Raj thought, lacked personality, was brimming with charisma that day.

The outcome of the meeting was good, since the clinicians agreed that they would make a concerted effort to complete more autopsies.

Though harassed at work and bored with life in general, the young Indian doctor was becoming financially more secure; Raj had substituted Kellogg's Corn Flakes for home-brand oats and bottled spring water for tap water. He also bought a car that one might call a jalopy, but it drove well and had air-conditioning—a necessity and not a luxury in the tropics. Raj usually parked his car next to his unit under a gum tree.

That day he took the pigskin briefcase that he had acquired from the markets to work, even though there was no obvious reason to do so. Maybe he wanted to show off the cherished possession; it was a bargain for twenty-five dollars, and he showed it proudly to Sarah when he walked in, who complimented him on it.

"Looks very nice," she said. "Dr. Stich has a similar one."

There seemed to be no increase in Dr. Stich's finances, though, for he stayed with home-brand oats, home-brand chicken stock, and tap water. Every two hours while he was at work, Dr. Stich would hurriedly march outside. Raj investigated the reason for this interlude, because he suspected his elderly colleague was going out to meet up with a secret belle. However, Raj discovered that Dr. Stich's short ventures were for far more mundane reasons. To avoid a parking fee, the older man parked his car on the roadside, and as there was a two-hour limit on roadside parking, he would move his car a bit forwards every couple of hours. He did this without starting the motor, since at the beginning of the day, he would park at the top of a hill, and then at the end of every two hours, he would coast downwards.

Sometimes Dr. Stich would be out longer than usual.

"Loo paper is on sale at Woollies," Sarah would say as she winked at Raj, obviously meaning that Dr. Stich had been out shopping to take advantage of an elusive discount. Back at home, people used to call Raj a miser, for various reasons, but when compared to the master miser, Raj was a spendthrift.

There was this favourite story of Raj's mother. A miser went to the guru of all misers to learn the art of miserliness. It was late in the evening, and the guru blew out the lamp. "Well, we've seen each other. To hear me, you do not need light, and that way you save some oil. This is the first lesson," the revered guru said. After a couple of hours, the guru had finished the day's class and took the match to light the lamp.

"Wait a minute," the student said. "Wait for me to dress before you light the lamp. I had undressed so that my dress would not be soiled."

It is said that the guru then got up and prostrated himself before the student, begging him to reverse their roles.

Sometimes when Raj was dictating a report, Dr. Stich would storm into the office and shout, "Why are you so loud? Are you deaf?"

These intimidations grew more frequent, but Raj stayed on. "I've survived the nuns," he thought.

Though his accent remained Indian, Raj started greeting everybody with "How are you, mate?" He tried to do this in one flowing word as the Aussies did, without much success.

It was while cutting sections from a breast tumour in Adelaide that his boss there offered Raj some advice. "I would do it like this," she said. Raj was very happy and left the work undone. "She said she would do it," he thought. The next day the lab assistant asked Raj as to when he was going to finish the work. It took a while for Raj to understand that his boss was advising him how to do the work when she said "I would do it like this" and not volunteering to do it.

Raj went to his office sometimes after office hours to finish off any pending work. He would sometimes see John wandering through the hospital corridors deep in thought. Since he worked in the wards on some days, he had a stethoscope around his neck. If they bumped into each other, most often Dr. Largebone did not greet him or even smile; he seemed to look through Raj.

It might have been a week after the American soldier's autopsy that Raj received a telephone call from John. The Indian doctor had gone to sleep after watching a late-night movie on SBS.

"There is an autopsy. Though it is your week, I'd like to come with you. It sounds interesting."

As usual Dr. Largebone's voice was clear and without emotion, its even tone cutting through the night like an ice-cold knife as Raj sleepily answered the telephone. The funeral was fixed for eight o'clock the next morning, and hence they had to do the postmortem that night.

Raj got dressed and hurried towards the postmortem room, taking the shorter route, which passed near the lightning-struck eucalyptus tree. The gnarled monster was silhouetted against the night sky, and he appeared to smile mockingly at the young doctor. As he passed the tree, Raj thought he heard a faint clang of bottles distinct in the silence of the night, and his heart missed a beat. At almost the same time, the chirp of the crickets ceased. From afar a dingo let out a long mournful howl, and a shiver went through Raj's body.

A heavy, cold hand pressed on Raj's shoulder from behind. His heart leapt. "How are you?" the owner of the hand said. It was Jack, the autopsy technician.

Raj felt angry at the ambush but relieved that it was a live person who was escorting him. He muttered, "I'm fine." Raj's tone probably made Jack rethink resuming the pleasantries, and he accompanied Raj to the postmortem room without making conversation.

The beautiful twenty-five-year-old lady on the autopsy table appeared thin and emaciated but seemed to be asleep and not dead.

"Sonia Gairdner had malabsorption and died," Raj gathered from the autopsy notes.

Dr. Largebone arrived, and soon the atmosphere became serious and businesslike. The autopsy was uneventful except that Jack, as usual, did minimum physical labour.

The organs were unremarkable to the naked eye, but when the slides arrived a few days later, and John invited Raj to view them with him at the multiheaded teaching microscope, the pathologists got a surprise. Every organ system except the gastrointestinal system was normal. It was when the English doctor put the slides of the small intestine under the microscope that the Indian doctor could not believe his eyes: the small intestine showed numerous small parasites within the glands.

"Strongyloidiasis hyperinfection," he muttered.

"Yes, I wondered if you would pick it," John said, emotionless.

Raj, though he was a trainee registrar here, had been a consultant pathologist in India before he arrived in Australia and did not like being tested by somebody of his own age, but he was proud he could make the diagnosis without referring. He did not continue with the conversation, but when he had finished viewing the remaining slides, he got up to return to his office.

"Thank you for sharing the slides." Raj was polite in showing his gratitude.

"It's my case, and now it appears John has hijacked it," the Indian doctor mused on his way back to his office. John had, in fact, got Maria to send the slides to himself, but Raj was not very much bothered, as he knew that the English doctor would now finalise the autopsy report and relieve Raj of the stress.

Hardly had the young Indian pathologist reached his office when John appeared at his door with the WHO Manual of Infectious Diseases and the patient's chart. He grabbed a chair from the corner, sat next to Raj, and opened a marked page in the book.

"Strongyloidiasis infection usually does not produce any symptoms in people with normal immunity. Strongyloidiasis hyperinfection occurs in immune suppressed people as in AIDS patients and those undergoing chemotherapy, and then it can be fatal." The doctors pored over the patient's chart. Many investigations had been done on Sonia Gairdner, including tests for AIDS. There was no evidence of immune suppression.

About a couple of weeks had passed since the autopsy on Sonia Gairdner, and Raj was in his office preparing to go home after winding up the day's work.

"Here's your article."

The Indian doctor looked up to see John standing as usual like an apparition at his door, holding a few sheets of paper that he handed over to Raj. There was a letter addressed to Dr. Largebone from the editor of the *Journal of Infectious Diseases*: "Your article 'Strongyloidiasis Hyperinfection in an Immune-Competent Person' has been accepted for publication." The next few pages were the copy of the article. John was very kind and had put Raj as the second author; Dr. Stich was the third author.

"That's your copy—you can keep it." Before Raj could thank him, Dr. Largebone had left. There was no way Raj could not appreciate the English doctor's work, for within two weeks of the diagnosis, he had had the paper accepted for publication, but for a fleeting moment, he wondered, "How could John have sent off the article for publishing without getting my signature?"

Raj put the article in his leather briefcase and left his office. On the way out, he met Dr. Stich, who was standing next to Sarah's office chatting to her.

"Heard about your article," he said.

The Indian doctor thought he could sense slight mockery in Dr. Stich's words, because, strictly speaking, it was not his article. Raj put down his briefcase.

"It's not my article. It's John's. He's been kind to include my name."

"That's fine, congratulations!"

"Thank you very much."

"Raj, could you spell *orcein* for me?" Sarah asked innocently to divert the conversation as she had correctly deciphered that Raj did not find Dr. Stich's comments amusing and was trying to help him. Orcein was a stain that they regularly used in liver biopsies, and Raj was sure she knew the spelling very well.

Dr. Stich looked at Sarah with surprise, and it was evident from his expression that he understood what Sarah was attempting to do, and without saying anything more, he quickly picked up his briefcase and left the department for home.

"Thank you, Sarah," Raj said.

"You're welcome," Sarah replied without taking her eyes off the keyboard as she continued typing. Raj paused for a minute before picking up his briefcase and walking out of the office. While driving home, the young doctor's mind went over what had happened that day. Getting a paper in his name was wonderful, even if he was only the second author, but Dr. Stich was becoming more and more intolerable. Raj knew that there was nothing he could do about it; he had to suffer it in silence until he got a job elsewhere.

He parked his car close to his unit as usual and had his dinner of home-cooked fish and chapattis, the flat Indian wholemeal bread, before settling onto the couch.

"I'd like to look at the article once more and have a read," Raj thought and opened his briefcase. To his dismay, the article had disappeared; instead, there were two recent medical journals and a couple of old magazines. The doctor read the cover of the first magazine. *Signal*, it read, and there was a photo of an airman painting the picture of a ship on the tail of an aircraft, which had, in addition, the swastika printed boldly on it. Raj turned to the first page and realised it was a Nazi propaganda magazine dated

July 1941. The other one was a German magazine, and though he could not pronounce the name, it said *Illustrierter Beobachter*, and on the cover page, it had the picture of Adolf Hitler voting. The doctor flicked the cover and opened the first page, finding within the magazine an envelope with a name written on the front, and, though the ink was fading, Raj couldn't believe it when he read "Dr. Freiderich S. Stich."

The young doctor instinctively opened the unsealed envelope; it was a letter written in German, and though he did not understand one word of German, the first line caught his attention: *Liebe SS.*

Raj's attention then turned to the last line: *Bezug.*

And then to the signature: *RR.*

Suddenly there was a rather loud knock on the door, and the young doctor dithered for a moment. The first knock was soon followed by a second knock, and this time it was much louder.

"Raj, are you there?"

Raj recognised Dr. Stich's voice.

The Indian doctor quickly put the envelope back in the magazine and then put both the magazines and journals back in the briefcase and closed it before opening the door. There was a fuming Dr. Stich on the doorstep with the devil's look in his eyes and his shorts fluttering in the wind like a rapid-fire machine gun. He held Raj's briefcase out to him.

"Why did you steal my briefcase?" the old man demanded.

"I didn't steal anybody's briefcase; instead, I think you walked away with mine. I thought the one that was left was mine, and, naturally, I picked that up and came home." Raj was calm when he made his reply to the allegation. Raj received the briefcase from Dr. Stich and took it to his room, where he picked up the older man's briefcase that he then handed over to him.

"Do you want to come in?" Raj invited Dr. Stich.

"No, and good night." Dr. Stich walked to his car, got in, and left. Raj shut the door and went back into the room, where he straightaway noticed to his horror that the letter addressed to Dr. Stich was still lying on the table. In his hurry he had forgotten to put the letter back in the envelope, and it was the empty envelope that he had put in the magazine.

CHAPTER 17

THE CURSE AND THE AFTERMATH

Time passed, and the wet season gave way to the dry, the only other season in the top end. It was about six in the evening when Raj parked his car near the beach.

There were two young couples at Cable Beach that day, probably in their early twenties, all of them naked and enjoying the privileges of the clothes-optional beach. The young men had erect willies, and the girls had firm breasts; the trees beyond the beach were green, and nature joined the small group on the beach in flaunting its youth.

"Come night they will make love on the open beach," the young doctor mused wistfully.

"Nature, including the human race, maintains its beauty by the death of the aged and the sick," he thought. "But not all the aged and the sick die; sick people like Dr. Stich and sick trees like the lightning-struck eucalyptus tree refuse to do so."

He stayed at the beach, enjoying the beautiful tropical sunset, the sky crimson red on the western horizon, the centre of which was adorned by the setting sun. The lord of the day, while bidding farewell, resembled an oriental dragon breathing its last gasps of fire before it drowned in its vast watery grave.

The ocean looked inviting, but Raj dared not go in. There were a few swimmers and about four surfers on the beach, all wearing full wetsuits, because of the stingers or the box jellyfish that northern Australian waters were infamous for. On the footpath parallel to the beach, a group of teenage roller skaters in vivid beach clothes glided past effortlessly, darting like gnats between pretty, skimpily clad yummy mummies pushing designer prams. Broome, the northern country town of the Western Australian desert, had a natural beauty and sophistication that any modern city would vie for.

Raj walked to his car and turned on the ignition. It did not produce the usual grunt from the jalopy. "Sometimes when these cars get old, they have this problem with the starting motor," a mechanic with an ancient, wrinkled, and toothless grin had told Raj in a kind voice when he had taken it to him for a service. This reluctance to start had happened a few times before, but the young doctor did not want it to happen now. He knew he could roll-start the car—a gentle nudge, and the motor would start working, but he was not going to push the car—no, not in front of the august crowd. Luckily, the car was on top of a hill, and Raj was hit with a brilliant idea. He opened the driver's door a wee bit, put his leg on the ground through the gap, and pushed. The car rolled forward and then hesitated for a moment, like an old bull pausing for a last fart before being taken to the abattoir, and then spurred into life.

Raj was not feeling well that night. The pain in his upper abdomen had been rumbling for some time, and tonight, after reaching his unit, it suddenly became severe. Sarah had mentioned again that his eyes looked yellow. He confirmed this in the mirror.

The phone rang. It was John, calmly announcing that there was an autopsy to do that night.

Elizabeth Peacock was a fifty-three-year-old white missionary from Ayers Rock, now known as Uluru, and had done a lot for the indigenous people, but sometime in the recent past, she'd got into trouble with one of the elders and was cursed for some reason, after which the missionary wasted away and died within a year. She had lost a lot of weight; in fact, on the autopsy table, she looked like an emaciated witch.

"She weighs twenty-three kilos," Frank, the autopsy technician, said as a statement of fact.

Weighing the dead bodies was one of the few things that the autopsy technicians did without being badgered; they never made one incision on the body, just as they never cleaned the bowel.

Elizabeth Peacock's skin was pasted tight on her thin emaciated body, her long aquiline nose resembling the beak of a mummified eagle. Her cheeks were sunken and hugged the contours of her teeth, and her eye sockets were two large and deep pits. Her fingers were thin, dried, and pointed, resembling the claws of a bird, and her breasts were shrivelled and plastered to her chest.

Raj decided to be firm with the autopsy technicians that day.

"Would you please clean the bowel for me?" His voice was clear and even-toned but not intimidating. As he expected, the technicians did not budge.

"I'd like you to please clean the bowel," he repeated. The Indian doctor's voice was slightly louder this time, and John, who was bent over the body, looked up, sensing tension in the air.

"What are you going to do?" Jack's question was more like a statement, implying there was nothing the young doctor, or, for that matter, anybody in the world, could do.

"I'm doing my work. The Royal College of Pathologists manual clearly states that the autopsy technician has to prepare the bowel for the pathologist to inspect. If you do not wish to clean the bowel, I shall record this in the autopsy notes and send a copy of it with the relevant page from the college manual to the hospital director. But I've no problems in helping you if you would clean the bowel."

The scoundrels looked at Raj with disbelief. Very seldom indeed did anybody dare tread on their feet; the last person who tried to interfere with their reign was Dr. Dumbbell, their previous boss, who ended up paying a very high price by hanging himself on the lightning-struck tree.

"You will pay for this," Jack muttered, before reluctantly starting to open the bowel.

"Please give him a hand," Raj said, looking pointedly at Frank, whose eyes betrayed reluctant submission as he moved to the side of the autopsy table to help his friend.

The bowel was opened, cleaned, and ready in fifteen minutes.

Elizabeth's organs did not reveal much, except that they weighed much less than normal; in fact, they weighed even less than one would expect for a person with such a low body weight.

The slides were ready within a week, and the two pathologists looked at them under the microscope. The features were typical of systemic sclerosis.

The medical textbook detailed the prognosis of the disease: "Systemic sclerosis is an immunological disorder affecting almost all the organs of the body, including the skin, gut, lungs, and kidneys when the body's defences attack the body itself. The clinical features include taut skin and marked difficulty in swallowing because of fibrosis of the oesophagus, or food pipe, and the affected patients lose weight, and their kidneys fail. The progress of the disease can be slowed with drugs, but the disease is relentless with an overall five-year survival of 70 percent."

"Why did they not diagnose Elizabeth's illness before she died?" The fleeting thought passed through the Indian doctor's mind after he had viewed the slides.

Dr. Largebone was seldom seen outside his office for a couple of weeks, and when Raj passed by his office, he saw John constantly bent on his computer keyboard typing.

"Five cases of systemic sclerosis" was the title of the article published in the *Journal of Immunology* by Dr. Largebone and Dr. Stich. John had pulled out four more cases of systemic sclerosis from the hospital records and had written this wonderful article.

CHAPTER 18

DEATH, BE NOT PROUD

Life is weaker than death, and death is weaker than love.

—Khalil Gibran

It was probably about five months after his arrival in Broome that Raj was again hit by stomach pain and jaundice. That evening he had a long swim in the pool. Normally the young doctor would restrict swimming to forty laps, two kilometres in total, but that day he was in high spirits, since Vidya had rung him saying she would be able to visit him soon, and he wanted to get back in shape. He did eighty laps of continuous freestyle, and though he became tired on emerging from the pool, he felt okay, but later in the evening he felt feverish and had a severe headache. His nose was blocked, and his throat hurt; he must have slept for only an hour or two before waking up with severe stomach pain.

Raj doubled up in bed because of the pain and wished for death, thinking anything would be better than enduring such severe agony. Raj yearned for Vidya's presence, but her research was at a crucial point, and she could not leave at that time; he had called her that morning, and she said she would come the next Sunday.

The young doctor bore the pain till early morning when, on realising he could not suffer it any longer, he somehow made it to the hospital emergency department and got himself admitted. There they investigated him thoroughly—he endured an ECG, ultrasound of the abdomen, CT scan, measures of blood calcium levels, and studies of pancreatic function. He was on sick leave for a week, and though he was treated with morphine and sedatives, the pain was still too severe. As he lay groaning in his hospital bed, help came from an unexpected quarter.

John was very kind to him, bringing Raj books to read and taking great interest in his progress. The Englishman would get the lab results each day and read them to Raj. Although Raj knew what the results meant, John, being the meticulous person he was, would explain in detail what each test implied, while the Indian doctor would listen with disdain, as he was sure he was going to die. The biochemical investigations showed that Raj had an obstruction of the bile duct, which brought bile from the liver to the small intestine. It could be due to various reasons, including stones in the duct or cancer of the pancreas, since the duct passed through the pancreas before it reached the intestine. However, Raj's scans were negative for any tumour or stone.

"We'll do a cholecystogram and an ERCP," Dr. James Lambert, the surgeon, said.

A cholecystogram meant injecting a dye into the gall bladder, the bag-like organ that collects and concentrates bile, using a catheter, and then taking x-rays to visualise the gall-bladder lumen. An ERCP was when they injected dye and visualised the bile duct and pancreatic duct. Raj underwent every investigation the doctors could think of, but they could not find the cause of the obstruction.

In about a week, the jaundice and the pain eased, and when he was discharged on the Friday afternoon, the young doctor returned to his unit and telephoned Vidya to tell her the good news. "I am flying tomorrow and should reach there by five in the morning the day after," she said. "Do not come to the airport if you are not well."

Raj felt much better when Vidya told him she was coming, but he was tired and soon drifted off into a deep sleep.

The next thing that Raj remembered was trying to pull the oxygen mask away from his face in the hospital bed.

He remained in the intensive-care unit for one more day, when Vidya was allowed to visit him.

It was only then that he learnt the whole story: his wife had reached Broome on Saturday morning instead of Sunday morning and found the unit locked with no response to her knocking. She rang her husband's mobile. When she heard it ringing from inside, she walked to the side of the unit, which is when she saw the broken windowpane and Raj lying in bed, blood oozing from his nose. Vidya went into hysterical fits, and a nurse from the next unit rang the ambulance. They paramedics got in using a master key and moved the young doctor to the hospital.

Carbon-monoxide poisoning as a result of a suicide attempt from car exhaust fumes was the diagnosis. There was a hose connecting the muffler of his car to the air-conditioning vent.

After two days in the ICU, the young doctor was moved to the ward, where he stayed for another two days, slowly regaining his senses. But he spent hours deep in thought, and whenever Vidya tried to start a conversation, there was not much of a response from her husband, which added to her chagrin and sadness.

The second day after being transferred to the ward, the young wife sat on her husband's bed, watching him intently. And then he started talking haltingly but clearly.

"I planned to fill the tank on Saturday—that means the tank was empty or almost empty."

"What do you mean?" Vidya appeared confused.

"Well, it means I did not gas myself. I wouldn't try it on an empty tank."

"I do not understand."

"Let me explain it to you. I didn't try to kill myself. Somebody tried to kill me."

"What?"

"Yeah, the assailant somehow got my key and started the car after attaching a hose to the exhaust, connecting it to the air-conditioning vent, not realising that the fuel tank was almost empty."

"Don't you think he would've looked at the fuel gauge?"

Raj smiled. "Well, in my car the fuel gauge always shows full, ever since I bought it. I put a little bit of petrol in it every Saturday."

"Ah...the broken fuel gauge saved you."

"Maybe."

"Who would want to kill you?" Vidya's voice was faint and halting, but her face betrayed emotions that revealed the painful thoughts that were passing through her mind. Although she was at first relieved that Raj may not have tried to kill himself, she found it hard to believe that somebody would try to kill her husband. She was livid with anger that such a thing could have happened; on top of that, there was a sudden rush of fear—a feeling that she had never experienced before when she pondered their future.

"I do not know. Anyway, I am here, and we are together. Yes, it is a miracle. I am alive because of a combination of events—the broken gauge, the broken window from the cricket ball," Raj stopped in midsentence, trying to think, and continued, "and your love."

Vidya got up from the bed and, moving to the window, stared at the horizon for a long time.

Raj was discharged the following day and allowed to go home.

CHAPTER 19

THE SUSPECTS

Pande durbala pinne gerbhini.
("She was already frail; on top of that
she has now become pregnant.")

"I am going back to India." Vidya was adamant.

"You will go back alone." Raj was surprisingly calm. *"Pande durbala pinne gerbhini."*

"What does that mean?"

"It means she was already frail; on top of that, she became pregnant. I was just trying to describe you."

"I'm not pregnant."

"I know you're not, but you act like a frail woman and, on top of that, who has become pregnant. Be strong." Raj was lying on the bed leaning on pillows, with Vidya sitting next to him, her chin resting in her cupped hands while she stared dejectedly at the floor. She did not reply to that insult for some time, but after a while, she looked straight into Raj's face and started a barrage.

"What are you doing here? Your boss does not like you; you almost got murdered, though even I am not sure if that really was a murder attempt. What are you trying to prove? Do you want to go back in a body bag?"

"Well, we do not know what is going to happen tomorrow," Raj replied. "If we run, where do we stop?"

"But here the odds are very much against you. Are you not scared?"

"I am scared. I fear for my life," Raj said. After pausing a bit, he continued, saying, "Fear is a manifestation of intelligence. If I say I'm not afraid, I'd be lying. But if I go back, I'd be a coward. The God who led Moses in the wilderness will save us, I am sure."

"But that God does not like the adventurous," Vidya tried to warn him. "And why did they have to walk for forty years when they could have reached the Promised Land in less than a year if they had walked straight?" Though raised as a Hindu, Raj's wife had accepted her husband's faith, and, in fact, she probably knew more about her new faith than did her husband.

"I can't agree with you on God not liking the adventurous. Didn't Jesus reach out his hand to Peter when he started sinking trying to walk on water? And the children of Israel…well, they walked through the desert a lot, and they suffered a lot. They defied the Lord and made their own idols that they worshipped. They turned their back on the same God who led them from captivity. Believe, and face your adversities." Raj paused before continuing. "Well, let me tell you. The person who tried to kill me wanted it to look like suicide. He most probably won't attempt it again because he failed and knows that we will be alert. If he had succeeded, I would have been in the long list of suicides in this country. Further, by staying here we may be able to discover who the criminal is."

"Whom do you suspect?"

"I do not know, though I would put Dr. Stich first on the list."

"Dr. Stich?" Vidya's face showed disbelief and shock. She stretched herself and sat upright. "But why?"

"Dr. Stich is a very complex personality; he has a few secrets." The young doctor then went on to tell his wife how the Saudi pathologist Iqbaal had bitched about Dr. Stich, and when he, Raj, had informed the elderly pathologist, his behaviour towards Raj had changed for the worse. He went on to relate to her the story of the journey to Derby to do the autopsy, the accident, and the box containing bags of white powder. Raj told her about the letter he had found in the car, signed by an SS saying that he was sending the stuff to RR.

"Who is this SS, and who is RR?" Vidya, now fully engrossed in the story, frowned and appeared deep in thought.

"Well," Raj continued, "I don't know who RR is, and I didn't know who SS was, until very recently."

The young lady looked at her husband's face, trying to fathom his thoughts.

Raj then told her how he had accidentally switched his briefcase for Dr. Stich's briefcase, the old Nazi propaganda magazines he had found in the briefcase, the letter in German within one of the magazines, and how a very upset Dr. Stich had come to his unit for the briefcase.

"SS is Dr. Stich—Dr. Frederic S. Stich." The envelope was addressed to Frederic S. Stich, and the letter started with the greeting "Liebe SS," or "Dear SS." Dr. Stich, I reckon, is known among his friends as SS—you know, the SS was the powerful Nazi army unit."

Vidya's gaze followed her husband as he got up from the bed and poured himself a glass of water from the fridge. He then walked to his wife and, clasping her head, bent over and kissed her on the forehead, before sitting down next to her. It was a few minutes before he started speaking again.

"Getting rid of me would be the best way to keep his secret."

"What secret?"

"Don't you get it? I believe Dr. Stich is a Nazi sympathiser, who is trafficking drugs."

"You mean the white powder was heroin?"

"Yeah, what else?"

"You must be reading too many crime novels."

"You still think I tried to commit suicide?"

"I don't know. If you think Dr. Stich tried to kill you, why don't you go to the police?"

"I don't have any proof to go to the police. Do you want me to lose my job? But I think Dr. Stich has the motive to kill me."

"Did you not tell me that he and the mortuary technician are enemies?"

"Yes, but he has used Jack as his courier. I can't explain this."

"Do you think you'll get the proof?"

"What proof?"

"That Dr. Stich tried to kill you."

"I might—in the meantime I want you to watch my back. We'll move out of the hospital campus."

"Who is your second suspect?"

"Well, the mortuary technicians, of course."

"Yes," Vidya agreed half seriously, half mockingly. "They have a reason to be angry with you, although I do not think they have a reason to get rid of you."

"Precisely, that is the reason why they are not first in the line of suspects."

"Who is the third suspect?"

"In my list of suspects, I would include everybody, including you, even though with your gentleness, you wouldn't even be able to kill a rat."

Vidya stood up and, walking to the wardrobe, got out her handbag, opened it, and took out something, following which she walked back to her husband and opened her closed fist revealing a couple of injection vials. He extended his hand towards her, and she gave him the vials, and the pathologist read out the labels, "Valium...insulin. Where did you get these from?"

"*You* should be telling me," Vidya stared at Raj.

"I don't know anything about these."

"I found them in your car. After the ambulance left, I wanted to follow it to the hospital. I got into the car. The key was in the ignition, and the ignition was on, but the motor was dead. I found that I could not start the car, although the fuel gauge was showing full. Then on the seat, I found these," Vidya said, pointing to the vials in Raj's hand. "I thought you had probably started using drugs. And when I got out, I saw this hose attached to the exhaust. Then I called the police. They came half an hour later. I forgot, or I did not want to give them the vials."

"Why?"

"Though I thought that the vials must be yours, I did not want the police to think that you were taking these. And what difference would it have made, anyway? The police searched the unit and locked it for further investigation. I had to move out for three days before they let me in. Meanwhile, they put some petrol in your old jalopy and drove it away."

"Why did you think I would be using insulin? I could be using diazepam, especially when one can't sleep with pain. But why did you think I would be using insulin?"

"You had obstructive jaundice, and one of its causes is pancreatic cancer or pancreatitis, both of which would also cause diabetes." Vidya's reasoning for her husband using insulin was rational and to the point.

"Well, I did not and do not use either of these," Raj replied, his face showing anger and sadness. "Maybe the assailant is a junkie." Raj stared at the vials of medicine and rolled them in his hand.

"Maybe it's not your boss," Vidya countered.

Raj rolled the vial in his hand and slowly drifted off to sleep. The vials of drugs rolled out of his hand and fell onto the bed. Vidya picked them up, put them in a small envelope, and returned them to the wardrobe, after which she came back and sat next to Raj on the bed.

Vidya was weary and felt helpless and angry, not knowing what to do or how to react, although she empathised with her husband. The project that she was doing in Adelaide was almost done, meaning the hard physical labour in the lab was over, and now all she had to do was to tabulate the results and do the write-up, which could be done in Broome. She knew for certain that she was not the weakling that Raj described her to be, for it had taken considerable grit and effort to become a lecturer at one of India's most reputable medical schools, but nothing in her life had prepared her for what she was going through now. She had come to Australia just for the heck of it; meanwhile, Raj had got this job, and everything had been going well. She had been cruising through her work when Raj rang and told her about the jaundice. Though Raj did not share his worries with her, Vidya knew the implications of obstructive jaundice, which includes stones in the bile duct or tumour of the pancreas, almost always killing its victims in a few months. To top all this, the murder or suicide attempt was something she could not bear. She trusted her husband and believed him when he said that it was a murder attempt and not a suicide attempt, but she was not sure if the painkillers and sedatives, which Raj took, would not have made him try to take his own life without his realising it. She would have been happy to go home to India now, as she would be among friends and relatives, but the young wife knew her husband was obstinate and foolhardy and would never give up in these extremely adverse circumstances. It never mattered to him whether he begged, borrowed, or stole; her husband seemed to always get what he wanted.

Vidya remembered how persistent Raj was in his courting her, a Hindu girl, even though marital relationships between the two communities were very uncommon. She had initially resisted his attempts earnestly, but the young man's perseverance had finally paid off, for not only did she accept him as her lawful wedded husband but also embraced his religion with such fervour that she studied Christianity deeply and became an ardent believer.

Vidya knew Raj would spare no effort to achieve the Western qualification that he had always yearned for, and it all seemed to be going their way till recently, but not even in her wildest dreams did she envisage these extremely unfortunate happenings. Vidya felt that her head was splitting, and, opening her briefcase, she pulled out the rosary that one of her friends had brought her from Lourdes. She then knelt beside her husband's bed and started praying.

CHAPTER 20

THE FIRST POLICE INTERVIEW

"You have to have an evaluation by a psychiatrist before you can continue working here," Raj was told in a letter he had received from the Director of Medical Services the day he was discharged from the hospital. "The hospital will bear the expenses of the psychiatrist."

The psychiatrist was a short, plump Indian lady of around forty, who, when she moved around, reminded Raj of a soccer ball played in slow motion.

Raj told the psychiatrist what had happened and his waking up in the hospital after the alleged suicide attempt. He went on to explain to her that the petrol tank was empty or almost empty at that time, and that contributed to his being alive.

"It's unlikely that one would attempt to gas oneself on an empty tank," the young pathologist concluded at the end of the monologue.

The psychiatrist sat in her chair gazing at Raj for some time without talking as if she was trying to reach into her patient's heart to assess his integrity. It felt like minutes passed before she reached across the table for the telephone and dialled the police.

"I've a bizarre case here. My protocol says you should take his statement first before I assess him." The psychiatrist then asked Raj to wait outside while she wrote a letter to the police.

There followed a lot of questions.

The Chief of Investigations was a young man in his early thirties named Raphael Montessori. He looked smart in his uniform. His cap rested on the table in front of him, and his gaze alternated between the cap and the young doctor. Raphael's longish hair was well oiled and plastered close to his skull, and his long nose and square jaw gave him a commanding presence that made Raj slightly uncomfortable.

"Do you have any reason to attempt suicide?"

"No."

"No, none at all?"

"No."

"Then tell me why did you do this?"

"Why did I do what?"

"Gas yourself."

"Gas myself?"

"Yeah."

"I did not gas myself."

"Your key was in the car ignition."

"Somebody got into my unit and stole the keys."

"Are you saying somebody tried to kill you?"

"Yeah."

"What are your reasons to convince us that this was a murder attempt?"

"Well," Raj began, "if I'd wanted to kill myself, I would've filled my petrol tank first and then gassed myself, rather than run the engine on a tank that was almost empty."

"Don't you think the assailant would have checked the fuel gauge?"

"Yes, of course."

"Then? You reckon the so-called killer is intellectually compromised to try to gas you on an empty tank?"

"He wasn't intellectually compromised, but my car was."

"Are you trying to tell me that your car tried to kill you?"

"No, let me explain."

"Please do."

"My car's fuel gauge is broken and always shows full, even when the tank is empty. I always put twenty litres in after every one hundred and forty kilometres, and I was going to fill it that Saturday."

The detective did not reply but sat there gazing at Raj for some time. Then he said, "As per our records, you were admitted to the hospital a few days before the incident with a history of jaundice and abdominal pain. Did you take any drugs to go to sleep?"

"I didn't, and why does that matter anyway?"

"I would like you to answer my questions."

"I have a right to know why I am being questioned."

"Because if you had taken sleeping pills, they might have made you forget that your tank was empty. Moreover, some of these pills are known to cause actions that are not really intentional. And your medical records say that you were on prescription pills to sleep."

"I remember taking some pills to go to sleep. Let me remember...yes, I took Stilnox."

"Stilnox is known to cause unintended behaviour."

It was Raj's turn to be surprised. He had forgotten that Stilnox could produce sleepwalking and sometimes bizarre behaviour, but he never expected the detective to be that knowledgeable. He mentally congratulated the policeman for his knowledge.

"Stilnox is known to cause actions that are unintended, such as jumping off a cliff, but I have not heard that it could cause or be responsible for complex unintended actions like a well-planned suicide," Raj countered.

"Well, you may not know, and probably this is the first incident. Do you have any suspects?" the officer asked.

"Yes and no," Raj replied. "I had a verbal altercation with the two autopsy technicians, and one of them muttered that I'd have to pay for making him work." Raj then related how he had made the ruffians clean the bowel. "I did not then—and even now do not—take that threat seriously, but if you ask me, yeah, I have them as suspects."

The interview did not last long.

"We'll see each other again," the officer said, shaking hands with Raj.

Raj's neighbours were later interviewed, and the occasional neighbour who was around at that time did not remember seeing Raj near his car after he was discharged from the hospital. In fact, none of them saw anybody within the premises of Raj's unit the night of the incident.

The autopsy technicians were questioned but later released as they had perfect or almost perfect alibis; Don Coward, the politician, was able to vouch that Jack was with him at the pub during that night and that he himself had driven him home. Jack's wife's testimony corroborated the evidence given by the politician, and Jack had spent the rest of the night with his family. Frank, the other technician, went to a concert with his girlfriend that night, and she vouched for him that he was with her the whole night.

Vidya had almost finished her project. "I'll go back, wind up everything, and return here within a week. If I have the data with me, I can finish the writing up from here. Maybe I'll have to go back once more to clarify some things."

She did not talk much those two days but was always with Raj till he saw her off at the airport.

CHAPTER 21

RAJ'S PREDICAMENT AND
THE SECOND ATTEMPT ON RAJ'S LIFE

Namboodiri pidicha pulivalu
("The tiger's tail caught by the Brahmin.")

Raj's mother told him this bedtime story:
Krishnan Namboodiripadu, a Brahmin, was a wealthy landlord, and Kesavon was his poor and often ill-treated tenant. Once a week, when he visited his uncle in the neighbouring village, Kesavon had to pass through a forest. One day, while on his way to see his uncle, a leopard jumped on Kesavon, but the agile villager sidestepped, and as the beast lunged past him, he grabbed at the animal. To his dismay Kesavon found himself grasping the leopard's tail, and when the big cat turned, the poor man clung to its tail for dear life and turned with the animal, and hence the hungry beast could not reach him. Whatever the animal did, Kesavon did not let go his grasp on the beast's tail. The poor man had some coins tucked in the waistband of his loincloth, and in the melee

the coins fell out. It was then that the rich Brahmin, Kesovon's landlord, came that way.

"What is this, Kesavon?" the landlord asked, surveying the scene. He first looked at Kesavon clutching the leopard's tail, and then his greedy eyes fell on the coins spread on the ground.

"Can't you see, my lord? This is the leopard that shits money. You just have to hold its tail."

Gladly, the Brahmin accepted the offer. Kesavon picked up his money and went on his way.

"By accepting this job with Dr. Stich," Raj thought, "have I been as foolish as the Brahmin?" He could not leave the job, as he did not have another one, and the only thing he could do was to hang in there.

Dr. Stich's attitude towards Raj continued to be hostile and caustic. One of his favourite pastimes was to stand in the doorway of Raj's office within ten minutes of his getting the day's work and innocently enquire, "Are you ready to show me the slides?"

Normally it would take a couple of hours to finish looking at the slides and another hour to get the report typed, but the young pathologist would somehow finish the work within an hour and put the slides and typed reports on Dr. Stich's table. In the hurry to do so, Raj would sometimes forget to get the previous references of an occasional case from the computer records. Dr. Stich would shout at Raj for these great omissions. Sometimes, after putting the slides and notes on Dr. Stich's table, Raj would suddenly realise he needed to make an alteration to one or two of the reports, and so he would creep into Dr. Stich's office to make the corrections, for he knew that Dr. Stich brooked no mistakes.

Most of the time, Dame Fortune would deal him a cruel hand, and Dr. Stich would notice the young doctor tiptoeing into his office, at which point the older man would raise his head from the microscope and shout, "Why are you here?" Raj would beat a hasty retreat without making the alterations, and finally at the time of checking the slides, Dr. Stich would again holler, "Why did you get this wrong?"

On these days of misery and solitude, the young Indian doctor sometimes biked to his elderly friend Joseph Varghese's house. Though he never told Joseph his worries, Raj found some solace and peace in his house. They sat on the veranda together, enjoying a couple of Victoria Bitters, the occasional *beedi*—a tiny Indian cigarette—and the beautiful food that Joseph's wife cooked.

Joseph's house was not far from the hospital. As he biked there leisurely that Wednesday evening, he tried to put his miseries behind him, but the young pathologist could not get his mind off the causes of jaundice in an adult. His biochemical investigations told him that the jaundice was probably of an obstructive nature, which, combined with the presentation of abdominal pain, was most probably due to a blockage in the bile duct that carries bile into the intestine. This block could be due to a stone in the bile duct or obstruction from outside, the commonest cause of which was cancer of the pancreas, a disease that invariably killed the victim in a few months, a thought that kept coming back to him the more he tried not to think about it.

The road had just two lanes, one in either direction, and Raj rode his bike on the edge of the road, as there was no cycle path. The road was almost empty, but the air was thick, humid and rich with the aroma of ripe mangoes splattered on the roadside. Bunches of flies covered the rotting mangoes, and they lifted off to attack the lone cyclist whose sweaty face they charged at in unison, like bees attracted to a single rose in the desert. There were dark clouds drifting across the sky, and the setting sun bestowed a bright crimson hue to the horizon.

Suddenly Raj felt a whoosh towards his right side, and he found himself almost pushed off the road by a car that brushed his shoulder. Before he could grasp what had happened, the bike hit the kerb, and he was flying through the air headfirst. The young man's outstretched hand cushioned the fall, and like a well-trained acrobat, he rolled and came up sitting on the grass. Raj looked up just in time to see a blue sedan disappear around the bend of the road.

CHAPTER 22

MARIA, THE TEMPTRESS

Raj was dishevelled but unhurt when he got up and slowly remounted his bike.

"Am I imagining things?" he wondered. "Was this deliberate or just a hoon driver?"

He had not seen the car's number plate, nor had he time to see what model the car was, and he knew very well that there was no point in complaining to the police without the registration number or the make of the car. Even if he had these specifications, the young doctor was well aware that as an Indian there was not much point in complaining after his experience with the police and the disinterest they had shown in the murder attempt on him.

Raj felt so dejected and tired that he decided against visiting his friend and turned the bike around. The handlebar was twisted, but he bent it back into shape and slowly biked back to his unit, where he had a shower and attempted to put his mind off the troubles of the day. Lying down on the couch with a Victoria Bitter, he rang his wife.

"There was a small incident today," he said. Slowly he related to her what had happened. There was a pause at the other end when he finished.

"Are you all right?" Vidya asked.

"I'm all right."

"It must be hoons."

"Maybe. Don't worry, anyway."

"Good night, kiss you."

"Kiss you too." Raj turned his mobile off.

The young man missed his lovely wife very much. Vidya had been away before, but this time the loneliness was more keenly felt. There was some solace, though, in the form of an exotic beauty. But while this brought comfort, it also brought more pain and distress, which Raj never anticipated or desired.

Maria often delivered trays of slides to Raj's office, and when she arrived, she would linger for a few minutes to chat. The young doctor often wondered if it was by chance that her skirt would brush against his body. Maria always enquired if the sections were up to scratch, and sometimes Raj would show her interesting cases on the teaching multiheaded microscope in the conference room.

The Eritrean girl's beauty was matched or surpassed by her wit and intelligence. Her cheerful demeanour lit up the atmosphere of the lab, and her joyous mood was infectious, and everybody, including the staff working in the other branches of the hospital pathology department, from haematologists to biochemists and microbiologists, enjoyed her presence. Maria was the life of every party, her laughter, charm, and beauty transcending age and cultural barriers.

Raj could feel her innocent affection towards him, and he liked her for what she was. Maybe they had common ground, both coming from poor third-world countries bogged down in graft and corruption. Maria, in addition, had experienced the horrors of war and famine, to which she lost family members, leaving deep scars in her young mind. On occasions she would relate some of these stories to the Indian doctor, who deeply sympathised with her, because for him the travails through which Maria had passed were alien and extremely sorrowful.

Maria's boyfriend was a Caucasian Australian man working in the mines on a fly-in fly-out basis.

It was Friday evening, and Dr. Stich had left, without saying good-bye, as was his custom these days, when Sarah came past Raj's office and said good night. John had left a bit early, as he had finished his work for the day, and there remained only a few scientists in the blood and serology lab, who were doing the evening shift.

The young Indian doctor himself was getting ready to leave and had got up from his chair when suddenly the door opened, and Maria, her bag hanging from her shoulder, walked in, also on the way out. The Indian pathologist was caught by surprise by the girl's sudden arrival without knocking.

"Hi," he said.

Maria did not answer but, instead, grabbed him and hugged him tightly. Her lips then closed on his, and she bit his lower lip. The young man was taken by surprise. He hesitated a moment but soon found his hands tightening around her, passion building in his pants as she pressed her hips against his.

Then Raj pushed her back. "No, we can't do this."

Maria's face lost its lustre; the passion in her eyes gave way to disappointment and sorrow. "I'm sorry," she said, her eyes welling up with tears.

"It's all right." Having said this, the young man moved towards her, grabbing her behind her neck and pulling her close. Her breasts pressed against his chest so hard that he could feel her heart pounding. Raj kissed her eyes and then her nose, and his right hand slid down and cupped her buttocks; Maria's face shone with lust, and she responded by hugging him ever more tightly. Raj's hand slid further down, and he started pulling her skirt up.

The Eritrean girl suddenly stopped. "No, we can't do it here."

It was only then that his sense of his surroundings and his own moral upbringing started to have the upper hand on his raw animal instincts, and he withdrew from her. The girl's skirt fell back, and she took a step away from him.

"I'm leaving for holidays on Saturday to Africa to see my relatives. Please wait for me—don't bother anybody else, only me!"

"Maria," the young doctor whispered, "please don't. Go away."

Maria turned around and left the room as quickly as she had come.

Raj walked to his table and sat down, his chin resting in his hands.

"Oh God, what is happening? I don't want this to happen." The taste of illicit lust was overwhelming and at the same time painful—painful because of the feeling of guilt that came with it, and like the forbidden fruit, the guilt made it all the sweeter.

The young pathologist slowly got up and, collecting his bag, left his office. As he walked to his unit, he slowly realised that he was, after all, able to resist temptation before it was too late, no matter how overpowering and alluring it was. Though on the one hand he felt guilt, on the other he had the realisation that the angels had guarded over him that day and protected him.

As he would in occasions like this, the young man turned towards his old and venerable friend, Mr. Cobar, the mountain.

There was both appreciation and caution on the revered old man's face. "Take care, young fella," he seemed to tell him. "Be vigilant, for your family is your most important possession. Protect it by all means."

But the young doctor did not have to worry much. The exotic beauty who tormented him did not come back to pathology. On her return from Africa, Maria left pathology and joined nursing.

CHAPTER 23

JOHN'S UNIT

Raj met his wife at the airport the next day. As he walked towards her, he felt that his movements were mechanical at first, but when he hugged her, he found that the flame was still roaring, and he embraced her ever more tightly.

"I'm glad that you came." The young man's words brimmed with enthusiasm and conviction.

"You look better," his wife responded.

"You look good too."

Raj's heart ached, and though he was unusually silent while they walked to the car park, he held his lovely wife's hand firmly.

"Why are you not talking?" Vidya, obviously noticing his silence, asked him while they drove.

"Nothing. I was thinking of moving house. The unit was temporary. We need to move outside the hospital campus."

"Well, I have some news, for a change." Vidya's tone conveyed enthusiasm, which made Raj turn and look at his wife quizzically.

"What is it?"

"I have been offered a trainee job in Adelaide."

"Wonderful! Why did you not tell me before?"

"With you facing so many difficulties, I wondered how you would take this."

"Take what?"

"The news of my getting a job."

"Did you think I'd be jealous?"

"No." Her answer lacked conviction.

"My darling, I'm happy you got this job. Once I finish here, I should be able to join you in Adelaide. When do you have to start the new job?"

"In almost a month's time."

That afternoon they looked in the community newspaper and found a townhouse in a suburb close to the hospital and called the agent, who let them have a look that same evening. They liked the house and put in an application then and there, and the agent was happy to let them lease the house. The young couple moved to their new dwelling the next weekend.

"How about putting in some security cameras?" Vidya was concerned for her husband's safety.

"Are you becoming paranoid?"

"I think they may be helpful."

Raj knew it would be useless to argue and that giving in to his wife's wishes would make her happy.

"I'll ring John, and he may help to install the cameras."

Though he was not friendly with the English doctor, Raj knew that Dr. Largebone had the skills for the job and would not hesitate to help him. As expected, John readily agreed. He came over the next evening, and they set to work immediately. The English doctor, as usual, was very methodical and did the work as though he had been doing this sort of thing his whole life. Within a couple of hours, they had installed the security cameras. Vidya wanted to ask him to stay for tea, but before they knew it, Dr. Largebone had finished the job and left.

"I shall make beef curry, and we'll take it to him," she said.

"Why do you think he likes curry?"

"He is from the UK."

"So what?"

"He should like curry."

"Okay."

When Raj met the English doctor at work the next day, he made an appointment to visit him at his house that Sunday evening. Raj explained to him that his wife wanted to make curry and naan for him to say thanks, and John readily replied that he enjoyed all kinds of curries, whether they be mild, hot, or extra hot.

"I shall be at home at seven in the evening," Dr. Largebone said.

Raj and Vidya took a bus from their house to the hospital, as the police had taken their old car away for forensic investigation. John's unit was on the hospital campus on the side opposite to Raj's old unit. As they walked past the hospital, they took the lane that went past the lightning-struck eucalyptus tree.

"I wonder why nobody cuts down that tree." Vidya was curious.

"Well, the tree is very old, but it is not near any building. Moreover, it is sacred to the indigenous people, and hence is protected," he told her, repeating what Dr. Stich had told him on his first day at the hospital.

They reached the English pathologist's unit at about five to seven and knocked at the front door.

"Please come in," John shouted from inside, and finding the front door unlocked, the young couple walked into the living room. The English doctor was in the bedroom changing after a shower. The living room doubled as Dr. Largebone's study, which was a picture of perfection with not one book or folder out of place. On a small table was an old Leitz microscope, and above the table was a shelf where several folders were neatly arranged and labelled according to organ systems. Next to the microscope on the study table was a large folder.

"You should learn from John," the young lady chided her husband, whose habits were a study in contrast to the Englishman's, with books, files, and magazines scattered everywhere, where one would have to search for hours to find something. Vidya was different, and after her arrival, their home had become much tidier.

While his wife sat on the lounge, Raj walked to John's study table to while away the time. He started flicking through the large folder and, to his amazement, found that it contained the records of all the autopsies the English pathologist had done, filed in chronological order. Dr. Largebone had photocopied the clinical records of each patient, to which he'd added the autopsy findings and references from various medical journals.

"How are you?" John asked as he came out of the bedroom; he had already dried and groomed himself and looked smart as if he were off to a formal dinner. The scowl on his face conveyed that he did not relish Raj's curiosity.

"Hi, here's the beef curry I made for you—please let me know if you like it." Vidya took the container from her bag and extended it to the English doctor.

"Thanks." His tone was formal and emotionless. As if by reflex, Dr. Largebone received the container from Vidya and put it on the study table. Vidya's gaze shifted from John to her husband, her expression conveying her wonderment at how a person could be so impolite.

Their visit did not last long, and on their way back, the young couple decided to take the route around the hospital. The rising full moon had lit up the sky behind Mr. Benjora Cobar, and the young man searched the grand old man's face, seeking help. Raj's relationship with Benjora was special, which he did not share with anybody, not even with Vidya, and today his serene old friend appeared as though trying to warn him of some unseen danger. Vidya gazed at her husband quizzically as he stared at Benjora but kept her thoughts to herself.

That night Vidya went to bed early, while her husband watched SBS television till eleven thirty, when he got up from the couch to go to bed. The young man paused awhile on his way to the bathroom, as he watched his wife with sadness and sympathy. She resembled an angel, he thought; sometimes she would stir in her sleep from a dream or perhaps a nightmare. Although they had expected difficulties, the young doctors were not prepared for such misery when they set off from India. They were well aware that life wouldn't be easy in a new place, especially a new country and that a Western country too, and they had prepared themselves for apathy, bossy behaviour, and some racism, but nothing and nobody had warned them before they set off that Raj's life could be in danger. "How would the police have treated the murder attempt if the victim had been a white person?" Raj wondered. He knew that the police did not believe him when he told them that it was a murder attempt, because, for them, Raj was a coloured immigrant from a poor country, whose rights were less important than those of the saltwater crocodiles. The Australian police did not have time to worry about a black fellow from the subcontinent—their budget did not have provision for this. Their job was much easier if it were a suicide attempt, and Raj himself sometimes wondered if he really had attempted suicide and forgotten about it. His circumstances could have led many a faint heart to kill themselves—he was constantly harassed by his boss; he had a serious, undiagnosed medical condition; and he was being treated with morphine and other sedatives, which had psychotic side effects.

Raj staggered to the bedroom and fell to his knees at the bedside, where he prayed, his tears flowing freely and soaking the pillow. About half an hour later, his mind was clear, and he was determined to fight.

His prayers appeared to have been answered, for the next Tuesday, John suddenly appeared at his door.

"I need your help for a moment," he said.

The Indian doctor was surprised, since Dr. Largebone was always self-sufficient and never seemed to need any help.

"How can I help you?"

"I need a drop of blood." The Englishman's reply again caught Raj by surprise.

"You can have a litre; why stop at a drop?"

"Well, I need only a drop." John walked into Raj's office, put a small kit on his table, and took out a needle.

Raj extended his thumb to Dr. Largebone, who dabbed an alcohol swab on it and then pricked it with the needle. John then squeezed a drop of blood onto a glass slide, following which he made a smear using the side of another slide.

"See you soon." The brief visit ended, and John picked up his kit and left the room.

About half an hour later, Dr. Largebone was back at the Indian doctor's office.

"Have a look at this." John handed him a microscopic slide.

Raj took the slide and put it under his microscope. He could not believe his eyes. The red cells were oval shaped instead of being perfectly round.

"Is this my blood?"

"Yes."

"My God, and I did not know." Raj paused for a minute before continuing. "And that was the cause of the jaundice…"

"Haemolysis wasn't the only cause," the English doctor cut in before Raj had finished.

"Well…" Raj was thinking aloud. "Yes, I had pain…severe colicky pain. Yeah, I had obstructive jaundice."

"Both haemolytic and obstructive jaundice—remember, you had a severe fever that day. Infection increases haemolysis in ovalocytosis and leads to sludge in the bile duct." John's explanation was like Agatha Christie's Poirot filling in the blanks of a murder mystery. "Biliary sludge is difficult to pick up on imaging. That is why your investigations were negative."

"I agree." Raj's face revealed his happiness and gratitude at the great pathologist, who had discovered the cause of his suffering. "Thank you very much," he said and extended his hand.

They shook hands, and without saying anything more, Dr. Largebone left the room and returned to his office.

The young Indian doctor felt relieved. His jaundice was not due to pancreatic cancer. Ovalocytosis was an abnormality that he could live with. Ovalocytosis, where the red blood cells are oval in shape instead of their usual concave shape, usually causes mild jaundice and is mostly asymptomatic. However, infections in people with ovalocytosis can lead to increased break-up of the red cells or haemolysis, leading to its breakdown product, bilirubin, increasing the jaundice. Increased bilirubin can lead to stones or sludge formation in the bile duct, leading to obstructive jaundice as well.

Raj picked up the office phone and dialled his wife.

"Vidya, I have good news for you."

CHAPTER 24

DR. STICH'S LAIR

Kaupina puscham vadipole ninnu.
("The tip of the g-string stood straight like a stick.")

"We shall pay Dr. Stich a visit," Raj said.
"But why?"

"We might find something interesting—maybe the remaining part of the hose used to connect the exhaust to the air-conditioning vent."

"You really must be mad to believe that the old man tried to kill you, that he is physically capable of doing this in the middle of the night. What excuse do you have to visit him?" Vidya asked.

"We'll go to his house and tell him we were passing by and thought of dropping in to say hello. We could invite him for dinner at our place."

"What're you planning to achieve? Do you think he would exhibit the piece of hose on his shelf? Are you planning vengeance and thinking of poisoning him?"

"I don't have any plans. I just want to see his place. We might come across something."

"Do you know where he lives?"

"Yes, he took me there once when we were friends."

Dr. Stich lived on the third floor of a city apartment overlooking the ocean.

The police had returned their car, and that Saturday at around four in the evening, the young doctors drove to the city and parked on the street outside Dr. Stich's apartment building. Raj rang his boss from the security door downstairs, and the door opened, letting them in. They went up in the lift. Dr. Stich looked very relaxed and was surprisingly friendly and polite. After shaking hands with both of them, he led them to the lounge.

"We were passing by and thought we would pay you a visit. And you have not met my wife," Raj explained.

Dr. Stich exchanged pleasantries with Vidya.

"I was having a drink—please join me," he said and, without waiting for an answer, went into the adjacent room to get the wine.

As they waited, Raj noticed that the lounge room was exceptionally neat and tidy, and the leather couch, the matching carpet, the timber entertainment table, and the bookcase looked classic with a hint of luxury, which he was not really expecting. The bookcase contained medical books as well as old classics and a set of *Encyclopaedia Britannica*.

Dr. Stich soon returned with an opened bottle of wine.

"Well, I'm off to Kenya next week for a project and will be away for a week," he told them.

Dr. Stich walked to the buffet and retrieved two wineglasses. While he was pouring the drinks, Raj's gaze fell on the paperback lying on the table: *Mind of Serial Killers* by Jonathan Livingstone.

"Here you are," Dr. Stich said, passing the glasses of wine.

"Thank you very much." Raj put the wineglass on the shelf, and just as the older man was passing the glass to his wife, the young man let off the loudest sneeze he had ever done, and the glass fell from Vidya's hand and shattered into a thousand pieces.

"I am extremely sorry, Dr. Stich." Raj's attempt at apology sounded as clumsy and crude as his actions.

Dr. Stich lost his cool and his polite demeanour. The façade of politeness, which he had carefully maintained that evening, shattered with the glass, and his concealed uncouth character revealed itself in a torrent of profanity.

"May I get a broom?" Raj asked.

"Of course you may, baby," the old professor retorted sarcastically.

Dr. Stich led Raj through the corridor to the laundry where the young man found a mop and, together with Vidya, cleaned the floor while an indignant Dr. Stich stared at them. The Indian doctor later thought that Dr. Stich then resembled the old, portly, overrated, and racist British politician called Winston Churchill. Raj returned the dustpan and mop to the laundry and, on the way back, decided to do a little exploration. Next to the laundry was Dr. Stich's bedroom, with the doors open and lights on, and opposite to the bedroom was a closed door. Raj turned the handle of the closed door, and no sooner had he opened it than he drew back in horror, a silent scream escaping his mouth.

A cobra with its hood raised was lying on the table next to the door, gazing at him, and the young man froze in his tracks, waiting for the deadly creature to deliver the fatal strike. The serpent lay there, unmoving as if contemplating whether to strike or not, and after a minute or two, the young doctor gained enough courage to fish out the pocket torch that he always carried around and shone it first on the cobra and then around the room. Next to the cobra was a three-foot iguana with its mouth open and tongue protruding, and there were, in addition, various reptiles, birds, and mammals in the room, frozen midmovement, some on tables and some on the floor. An eagle in full flight hung from the ceiling in the centre of the room.

Raj then directed his torch onto the walls and saw to his surprise weapons of various descriptions hanging there. There were cutlasses and battleaxes, samurai swords and nunchucks, and daggers and lances; there were also modern weapons, including a shotgun, and various crossbows, but the thing that took his breath away was a hangman's noose, hanging from an auspicious position in the centre of the wall.

There were footsteps in the corridor—footsteps of heavy, bare feet.

"Fuck you! Who asked you to snoop around?" Dr. Stich looked as though he was on the verge of murder.

"I…I'm sorry. I lost my way."

"I knew you'd lose your way. Anyway, now you can get out."

The young couple made a hasty retreat, not only from the corridor and study but also from the apartment.

"*Kaupina puschan vadipole ninnu,*" Raj muttered as they ran down the stairs.

"What does that mean?" His wife was curious as usual.

"*Kaupina* means 'G-string,' *puscham* means 'the end,' *vadipole* means 'like a stick,' and *ninnu* means 'stood.'"

"I don't get it."

"It means that we showed a clean pair of heels. Well, in Kerala, in olden days, people used to walk around in G-strings. The central long piece of cloth that covers the crotch is taken between the legs and tucked under the waistband at the back, and the end hangs down like a tail. If one runs very fast, the tail will stay horizontal like a stick. Well, it just means that our retreat from Dr. Stich's lair was very hasty and not a glorious one."

They were soon outside the building, and Raj then explained to Vidya what he had seen in Dr. Stich's house.

"Interesting. Dr. Stich is certainly a man of many talents," she commented.

"He certainly is. The house's got one lounge with dining, one bedroom, and one study. On first glance, there is nothing that makes me suspicious. Dr. Stich collects weapons and is passionate about taxidermy. He probably has killed all those animals, but that won't make him a murderer. We'll go to the hospital. I want to have one more look at the spot where I parked the car that night."

They drove back to the hospital and parked at the hospital car park. As they started walking to their old unit, a blue sedan passed them and turned into the lane leading to the swimming pool. For obvious reasons, Raj's gaze followed it.

"Let's follow the car," Raj said.

Vidya did not ask why, but they quickened their pace and turned into the same lane that the car had turned into. A blue commodore was parked in the swimming-pool car park.

CHAPTER 25

THE BLUE CAR

"We'll wait here for the owner to return," Raj said.
"Why?"

Raj had told Vidya over the phone about how a blue car had screamed past him, forcing him to hit the kerb, toppling him from his bike. He again recounted to her the incident.

"It was a blue sedan. It might have been an accident, but I think it was deliberate. I just would like to see who drives this car. Maybe we'll go to the pool and check on the people who are swimming."

There were three swimmers in the pool—two women and a man—all of them with goggles on, so Raj could not make out who they were. The young doctors sat on the bench near the pool and waited for about half an hour, during which time a young couple came to the pool in their bathers and started swimming. Then one of the people who were already in the pool got out, a woman of about twenty, whom they did not know. Soon the man too got out of the pool. It was Jack Heath, the mortuary technician, and he walked towards them with not a very friendly expression.

"How are you going?" The typical Australian greeting was laced with sarcasm. "Are you waiting for me?" he added in a mocking voice.

Raj did not know what to say, for he had not expected Jack to be there.

"I like the colour of your car." That was the clumsiest reply in the circumstances, but that was all Raj could think of.

"So you followed the car like a butterfly chasing a flower."

"The butterfly does not have to chase the flower, as the flower stands still." Just like a cornered snake, Raj knew that attack was the best form of defence.

Jack turned and started walking away.

"Are you not going to the police with the new evidence?" Vidya asked.

"What evidence?"

"Did you not say that a blue car tried to kill you?"

"You are a funny girl."

"Well, you've a lot of clues now. The police will follow them up."

"The police will laugh at me. We don't have any proof of anything. I don't have a witness who would vouch that the car was blue. You see, Jack has an alibi—Don Coward vouched for him. He said that Jack was with him in the pub that night, but I think Don Coward is a racist, and he might have lied."

"What are you going to do?"

"For the police, the colour of the car is not enough. They'll need the model and the registration number. I'm not going to lie to the police that I'd noted the number down. When I was edged off the road, I didn't see the car clearly enough to even see the model, let alone the number plate. Anyway, I'm going to investigate Jack. I've seen him driving another car before, a white Daihatsu."

"This may be his wife's car. Until now you thought your boss tried to kill you. Do you still think that?"

"Dr. Stich is still my prime suspect. But I've never completely stopped suspecting Jack."

"You said you even doubted me. Do you doubt yourself?"

"Sometimes I do, and I'm investigating myself even though I'd not told you."

Raj then told Vidya how the drug Stilnox, which he had taken that night, could affect behaviour. "There have been instances of people jumping off cliffs after taking Stilnox," he said.

Vidya looked at Raj in some alarm. "This is news to me. Why did you not tell me before? I think we should go home."

"We are going home," Raj replied.

"Not this home but our home in India."

"Don't be a sissy. And what about your job in Adelaide?"

"I am not a sissy. If I were one, I wouldn't have come here. But I don't feel we are going to achieve anything staying here. We're in hostile territory. Nobody wants to buy your story of murder attempts. I don't want to continue to live in this country, even with the Adelaide job."

"What do you believe? Do you think I tried to gas myself?" Raj looked at his wife intently.

"I believe you."

Raj did not think there was conviction in his wife's words. But he did not say anything and let the argument lapse.

"I'm going to snoop around Jack's house when he is not there. Maybe I can get into the house and have a look also."

"Why don't you check if he is diabetic? Remember the insulin vial that was left behind in the car? If so, you have added evidence that he's the culprit."

"Added evidence that he *could* be the culprit," Raj corrected her. "How do I do that?"

"Punch his name into the lab results in the hospital computer, and see what results come up."

"Sounds fine; we'll try that. Hope nobody checks who tracked his reports." Her husband nodded with appreciation even though he knew it would be wrong to do it. All hospitals have tracking records of who visits various files, and even though he was a doctor at the hospital, it was illegal for Raj to visit records of a patient with whom he was not officially involved.

They walked to Raj's office in the lab, and he punched "Jack Heath" into the computer.

"Well, you might need the date of birth," Vidya murmured, standing behind Raj.

"I don't have his date of birth. But I don't think there are many Jack Heaths in Broome."

There were three Jack Heaths. The first one was aged twenty-two, the second fifteen. The third was aged forty-six.

"I think he is our Jack," the young doctor muttered. Unfortunately, Jack was not diabetic, his fasting blood sugar, recorded almost a year ago, being within normal limits. For no apparent reason, Raj went back to the search page on the hospital records and punched in just "Heath," leaving the first name and sex blank, and resumed the search, with Vidya watching. There were two pages of Heaths, and he checked their first names and ages, finally deciding to investigate a Margaret Heath, aged forty-five. Raj clicked on her pathology results; she was a diabetic on insulin and was under constant monitoring.

He looked at her address: "45 Cousin Street, Winston."

Raj clicked out of Margaret's record and went back to Jack Heath's, whose address also was 45 Cousin Street, Winston.

"We've something here!" he exclaimed.

"Well, I think I understand. You mean the insulin I found in the car must have been from Jack, who was taking it to his wife," Vidya joined in.

"Maybe—but let's not jump to any conclusions. We don't know who the assailant is. We're looking for leads or clues, and then we'll follow them up."

CHAPTER 26

THE INVESTIGATION OF
JACK HEATH'S HOUSE

"Jack's wife is a schoolteacher. I don't know if she works every day of the week."

Looking out through the window of his bedroom, Raj could make out Benjora Cobar, silhouetted against the dusky sky, but the young man could not fathom his older friend's emotions from so far away. He appeared neither to approve nor disapprove of what Raj was doing, saying, or thinking.

"I don't think you should snoop around Jack's house." Vidya was not sure this was a good idea, and she tried to dissuade Raj.

"We'll just ride past their house in the evening, and if they are out, we might be able to look around."

"What're you going to look for?"

"I don't know. Maybe the piece of hose that matches the piece that connected the car exhaust to the air-conditioning vent. Maybe vials of drugs, like diazepam, although I don't think he injects drugs."

"You said you were looking for a junkie."

"I don't have a clue who the criminal is. I'm just following my instincts, which I feel will perhaps lead us to the person behind this."

The following day, Raj and Vidya rode their bikes past Jack's house, which was one street away from the beach, at around eight in the night. The mortuary technician lived in a single-storey house with a large lawn out the front, and as they rode past, they saw a blue commodore parked in the carport and, through the window, a woman pottering around the house. Raj and Vidya did not stop there but kept on riding.

"Jack's wife is there," Vidya said, looking over her shoulder.

"Yeah, we can't go in if somebody's there," Raj replied.

They rode past Jack's house several following nights, and there were always two cars in the carport. Finally, they were lucky on Friday night when they found only one car parked in the carport, the white Daihatsu. The house was dark, and it appeared there was no one inside. Raj and Vidya kept on riding past the house and stopped at the next bend in the road, where they leaned their bikes on the fence near some bushes.

"You stay here," Raj told his wife. "First I'll check if I can find a way into the house from the backyard. If a car turns into the driveway, I'll get out. Meanwhile, you just stand here behind the bushes and give me a buzz if you see a car turning in."

Before his wife could say anything to dissuade him, the young man had left her there and walked to Jack's house, where the street was not well lit. He walked along the driveway and entered the double carport. The young man shone his torch around and found a gate at the back of the carport leading to the backyard. He soon found the back door of the house, but before touching anything, Raj pulled out a pair of surgical gloves from his pocket and donned them. He turned the handle and found that the door was not locked. The doctor-turned-sleuth quickly entered the family living room and kitchen, which, in turn, led to a corridor. There was a wooden pull-down staircase leading to the attic in the corridor close to one wall. The corridor opened into three rooms, the first a bedroom that, on entering, Raj noticed, had children's toys scattered around. Raj quickly exited and entered the next bedroom, which appeared to be the master bedroom, where, in the beam of his torchlight, Raj saw a dressing table next to the bed. The young man opened the top drawer and saw some papers in the drawer, which were mostly grocery bills, but there were a couple of bills from the garden shop and three bills from the hardware shop, which he stuffed into his pocket. The other drawers contained family photo albums and some women's toiletries.

Raj left the bedroom and walked back to the living room and kitchen. His mobile phone vibrated, and the young man grabbed it and looked at the number. It was Vidya.

"Hello, I'm fine," he said.

"I'm fine here also," Raj heard a muffled reply.

Raj put the phone back in his pocket and shone the torch around. Opposite to the door through which he had entered the bedroom, there was another door that led into a smaller room. No sooner had he moved across the bedroom to the door of the smaller room than he froze, hearing a woman's low moan coming from that room. He paused for a minute when he heard the moaning again; this time gasps interrupted the moaning, which cracked and sputtered towards the end like a woman's dying breath. Slowly Raj moved to the side of the wall and crept along the wall and peeped into the room, his torch beam making an arc inside the room that looked like a study with a writing table, a chair, and shelves on the wall. There was nobody there, but suddenly a blood-curdling scream rose from the room, and Raj took a hasty step backwards. The beam of his torch fell on the computer screen on the writing table, and then a different set of noises started coming from the computer; this time it was the deep bark of a greyhound. A bead of sweat fell from Raj's face to the ground. The torch beam fell on a mirror, and Raj was startled by his own reflection. He put his hand on the computer mouse and moved it, causing the screen to spring to life with an image of Jack and his wife smiling at him.

Suddenly Raj became aware of the sound of a car entering the driveway, and the mobile phone in his pocket vibrated, but this time the young sleuth did not answer it. The beam from the headlamps of a car flashed into the room for a moment, and as Raj looked out, a large car pulled into the carport and stopped with a grunt. In four long strides, the young man was in the kitchen, but it was clear that it was too late for him to get out, as, to his horror, he could hear children's voices in the backyard. Raj moved fast into the corridor and was up the ladder and into the attic just before the back door opened and the children burst in with excitement and laughter. The young sleuth could hear Jack reprimanding the children for being loud. The attic was full of cobwebs, and as Raj crept away from the attic door, his hand fell on something smooth and in a coil. The young sleuth felt around and then shone his torch on the object—a length of garden hose. Raj could hear Jack asking the kids to have a shower. The young man fished a pocketknife from his pocket and cut a small piece of the hose about three centimetres long.

He got his mobile phone from his pocket and rang Vidya.

"Where are you?" she asked.

"I'm all right. Please bike back to our house. I'll join you in an hour," Raj whispered.

About an hour later, at half past ten on Raj's watch, it seemed the house had become quiet, peaceful, and dark. The young man took his shoes off and climbed downstairs into the corridor and crept along the wall. Soon he was out of the house and in the backyard. He moved into the carport stealthily, but before leaving Raj thought he should have a look in there and shone his torch around. The couple's cars were there, and arranged along the walls were shelves with tools and boxes containing nails and screws. The beam of light fell on a cardboard box that, for some reason, Raj felt appeared familiar to him, and he pulled it out of the shelf. *Thump, thump.* The young sleuth felt his heart beat as he opened the cardboard box. Within it were small plastic bags containing white powder, and instinctively he grabbed one of the plastic bags and put it in his pocket.

He quickly walked to the front yard and, keeping to the shade of the garden plants, snuck along the road, soon reaching the bushes where he had hidden his bike.

CHAPTER 27

THE WHITE POWDER AND
THE PIECE OF HOSE

R aj reached his quarters about half an hour later, where his anxious wife was waiting for him. The young man gave her a brief account of what had happened. Vidya chuckled when she heard about the moaning computer.

But she also chided him. "Raj," she said emphatically, "I cannot approve of this. You cannot put yourself at risk doing this. If you are caught, you will be charged for criminal trespass, and all your hopes will be extinguished."

"I know you don't approve, but I have to find out who tried to finish me off. See what I've got." Raj fished out the hose piece and the plastic bag from his pocket and put them on the table.

"Everybody has a garden hose," Vidya said.

"Yes, I know that. But not everyone would have a garden hose that matches the hose used to try to murder me. And you don't usually store a garden hose in the attic unless you want to hide it."

Vidya picked up the hose piece and inspected it. "The size, I mean the diameter of this hose piece, is large enough to fit the muffler of your car, but I don't even remember what colour the original one was. It's with the police," she said.

146

"I'll have to see it, to check if it matches with this."

"You can't. Then you'll have to tell them where you got this from."

"Well, I'll have to ask them to show it to me. I'm sure they still think that I tried to kill myself. If it's similar to the hose that I found, I may have to tell them that I trespassed on Jack's property."

"But what's this?" Vidya asked a moment later, pointing to the plastic bag.

"Do you remember the accident Jack and I had while on the way to Derby to do a postmortem?" Raj asked.

"Yeah, I remember that."

"You remember my telling you about the cardboard box that was thrown from the car, littering plastic bags containing white powder?"

"Yes, you thought the bags contained heroin. Is this one of them?"

"Yeah, the box and the bag look very similar to those that were thrown out of the car."

"You said you got it from the garage shelf. You don't store contraband on a garage shelf. I remember your telling me that there was a letter in the car, which you later found was from Dr. Stich."

"Yeah, I agree." Raj walked into the bedroom and came back wearing white latex gloves.

He slit the bag and poured some of the contents onto a piece of white paper. It was a fine white powder. Raj took a pinch and, holding it near his nose, smelled it.

"It's got a mild waxy odour. I don't know the smell of heroin." Raj was feeling terribly sleepy. "Shit, I am tired. Let's go to bed and worry about the powder tomorrow."

The next morning Raj got up somewhat late at nine in the morning, and to his surprise, Vidya was nowhere to be seen. He tried ringing her mobile, but she had left it back at home, so he made himself some toast and coffee.

"Maybe she went for a swim," he thought. He took the bag of white powder and played with it awhile, wondering what it was, before getting up and having a shower. It was almost ten in the morning when Vidya returned, and as soon as she came in, she started working in the kitchen without even bothering to answer Raj's questions as to where she had been that morning.

"Give me some time," she said.

Raj noticed that the bag of white powder, which had been on the dining table, had disappeared, but he dared not go into the kitchen or ask Vidya if she knew where it had gone. Whenever Vidya asked him to keep away, she meant it, and Raj knew he had better stay put, so he sat in the living room, as he often did, surfing TV channels.

An hour later, Vidya called out from the kitchen.

"Look here," she said.

There was a blob of slime in the pot that she was cooking in.

"Is that lunch?" he asked.

"Don't you think of anything other than food? Your white powder is not heroin. It is borax."

"Borax?"

"I searched white powder used in taxidermy on the Internet, and it says borax."

"Why taxidermy?"

"Well, your boss is interested in taxidermy. He sent white powder through his technician to somebody in Derby."

"Good deduction." Raj's face showed he really appreciated Vidya's intellectual prowess. "Fantastic, really great, I really appreciate this. You are not just a pretty face." Raj was thoroughly pleased, and he gave his wife a hug. "So you did some experiments to prove it."

"Yeah, the net again helped me. I found out the chemical reactions of borax and came upon making slime from borax and polyvinyl alcohol."

"So that was where you disappeared to this morning—to buy polyvinyl alcohol. You could've told me."

"Well, you would've laughed at my theory."

"You are right. A woman's intelligence is not always appreciated." Raj's words echoed his sexist convictions. He paused before adding as an afterthought, "Why are they so secretive about this, my boss and Jack?"

"It might have been a hobby or even an illegal side business they have been carrying on for a long time. Killing native animals is illegal, and if they are trading the stuffed animals, I believe it is a greater offence. You are an outsider, and obviously they want you to remain like that. But at least now you know that neither your boss nor your friend Jack trafficked drugs."

"I agree with that, but that does not mean I should take them off my suspects list."

"Raj, I think this's getting too much. I'm going crazy." Vidya's voice faltered and ended in a sob.

"I know this is difficult. But you should know we must not and cannot run. I've not told you that I survived the nuns in primary school. Many of my classmates did not."

"What happened? Are they all dead?"

"Yeah."

"What do you mean?"

"Many schools in Kerala were run by tyrannical nuns, who vented their anger and frustrations on the hapless kids."

"What?"

"You have heard about priests, but nobody talks about the nuns. In fact, nobody seems to know how they satisfy their cravings."

"Stop it!" Vidya would not have any of this. Though she was born in a Hindu family, her faith was Christian, and she viewed Raj's comments as blasphemy.

"Well, I'll tell you what happened." Raj then related to his wife how the nuns used to punish their students severely for the silliest reasons. "Sorry, I still feel the pain, and that is the reason I am harsh about them. However, I agree they might have done it because they believed it was good for the kids, but, in fact, the effect is just the opposite. I agree they are not that evil." He continued to narrate to Vidya the rest of the story, how he had followed the nun into the chapel and his own experience there.

"No, I am not blaming them," he continued. "The narrow-minded society is the one to blame. Many of the children who studied in my school became antisocial and rowdy. Many became emotional wrecks. I escaped. I'm one of the only ones in my class who has succeeded."

Raj's eyes welled up with tears, and his speech was broken when he added slowly but with conviction, "I have forgiven them, including Sister Angelica."

Vidya listened intently, the expressions on her face changing from disbelief to surprise and intense sorrow. She got up at the end of the story and poured herself and Raj a stiff whisky. She sat on the couch next to Raj and looked through the window into nothingness and slowly sipped the alcohol.

"How did you succeed?"

"I do not know. Maybe it was my tenacity, or maybe because my mum taught me that nobody can take away my future, and only I—yes, only I—am responsible for my fate." Raj stopped for a moment before continuing. "Maybe my fear of the Lord who created the stars and the universe around us and also me and you in his own image. Maybe the Son, Jesus, who constantly begs His father, our Lord, to give me one more chance in spite of my imperfections. I don't consider myself to be more intelligent than any of my classmates. What I mean is that I—we—can withstand this and may be able to get to the bottom of this. Anyway, I have to compare the hose piece with the piece that the police have."

Vidya got up and, opening a drawer, pulled out a Bible and read aloud.

"Even if I walk through the valley of darkness, I shall not fear, for your staff and rod comfort me."

They went to the movies that afternoon, and on Sunday they attended the church service.

"Dear God, who sent His own Son for our sake, please help us," Raj prayed.

After mass was over, they drove to the mall for lunch.

"Vidya," he addressed his wife, "you know how we are special, how we should be special in the way we behave, think, and act? Sure we may go wrong, we may make mistakes, but we always have to believe that we are different, and there are very special and specific roles for us. We cannot run away. We may not always succeed. But if we do not try, we will never succeed. They may say hi to us, but the Aussies think we are vermin from the third world. We will show them we are good, and we will prevail."

CHAPTER 28

THE SECOND POLICE INTERVIEW

Raj rang Raphael Montessori, the chief of investigations in his case, the following Monday. The officer was very courteous on the phone, but the young Indian doctor knew that Raphael's attitude did not mean much and that his case would have been pushed to the bottom of the files because he was a coloured foreigner. Had this case been that of a white Australian, it would probably have made the headlines in all the newspapers.

Raphael promptly gave Raj an appointment. "Come to my office tomorrow at eight o'clock, mate."

It was pouring with rain when Raj and Vidya drove to the police station. Raj parked the car, with its front facing that of another car.

"Well, that guy forgot to turn his lights off," Raj commented, pointing to the headlights of the car facing theirs.

Though they both had umbrellas, they were drenched in the monsoonal downpour by the time they walked into the police station.

"What's up?" Raphael asked after exchanging pleasantries.

Raj took the hose piece from his pocket and showed it to Raphael.

"I found this near my old unit," he said, hoping that Raphael could not tell he was lying. "I went there last weekend looking for clues."

"How come we didn't find it?" Raphael's voice expressed some concern. Maybe he was worried that his police force was not systematic enough.

"This was in the bushes."

Raphael got up and went to the back door.

He returned with a piece of hose. Raj put his hose piece next to it. They were of the same size but were of different colours.

"All right, I'm wrong." Raj stood up. Raphael extended his hand. There was an embarrassed smile on Raj's face.

Raj walked out of the police station feeling dejected. He mulled over Vidya's advice to go home to India. There was abject poverty in India, and there were roads with chaotic traffic, which killed hundreds, but there you had a sense of belonging. Here everything appeared beautiful—the manicured lawns, the beautifully paved roads, and the wonderful malls—but it was clear that you did not belong; nobody seemed to be bothered even when someone had attempted to murder you. Raj knew this was so because he was not one of them but was just a poor black fellow from a third-world country, and they did not want to believe his story. For them, there was far less work to be done if they put the case down as a suicide attempt. They were simply apathetic.

They walked with bowed heads to the car. There was a slight letup in the rain.

"I told you, his battery has gone flat," Raj said, pointing at the car parked opposite to theirs. There was no glow in those headlamps. They slid into their jalopy, and the young man turned the ignition, but there was only a low grunt from the old motor, followed by silence. He turned the ignition again, and this time there was complete silence, not even the reluctant grunt. There was an old couple getting into the car opposite theirs, and while they watched aghast, that car's engine purred into life and started reversing. Raj fiddled with his own headlights by instinct.

"I think our lights were on." Raj's tone was subdued, almost apologetic. "It was our lights reflecting in their headlamp."

"And you are the super sleuth catching a killer," Vidya retorted without batting an eyelid.

Raj did not reply to that but got out of the car, this time not even bothering to take his umbrella, and it was a dripping wet man whom Raphael encountered at his door.

"What did you bring this time?"

For Raj, it was not a time for banter. Luckily, the police station had a battery pack, and Raj was able to jumpstart the car.

They stopped at the hospital.

"You can drive home; I'll be a while," Raj told Vidya. After she had gone, the young man walked to the hospital café and bought himself a coffee. On the way to his office, Raj glanced at the noticeboard outside the café, where people put ads for selling things, as he was on the lookout for a study desk for Vidya. There were no ads for desks, but somebody was selling a car, $2,000 or closest offer, for a 1992 Holden. The young man's eyes fell on the picture of the car, which did not seem to be in good nick. For some reason he kept on staring at the picture. Slowly the reason for his unusual interest dawned on him. The colour of the car was sky blue. He took out his phone and rang the number.

"If you want to have a look at it, come to Thirty-Two Gugeri Street, mate. My name is Nick."

"How many kilometres has it done?"

"Over two hundred thousand."

The person at the other end of the phone sounded Irish. He voice also had a certain quality, a quality that proclaimed lassitude or, even more, a sort of carelessness and vagueness.

"I shall let you know when I can come take a look at it," Raj said.

Raj was interested in the car, but he was more interested in the car's owner.

He quickly Googled the value of the model. Six hundred dollars was the recommended price.

The young doctor walked home that evening. Vidya was there, but the reception he got from her was far from enthusiastic. She seemed to be worried, and when he related the new developments to her, she appeared to show little more than passive interest.

"Are you going to chase every blue car in the country?" Vidya asked after a while.

"You are right; this is a wild goose chase, but this is the last one, I can assure you of that. But there is something odd about this car. The asking price is too high for the model and the kilometres it has done. I would like you to come with me tonight."

"Where do you want to go?"

"We will go to this guy's house and see if we can have a look at the car, and if we get a chance, we will also look inside his house."

Vidya was not enthusiastic, but with Raj's persistence, she finally gave in and agreed to go with him.

CHAPTER 29

THE BLUE CAR AGAIN

They set out at around eight at night on their bikes. They rode, because Raj thought it would be easier to hide their bikes than their car. The night was warm and still. There was no breeze, and even for Broome, it was damp; for some eerie reason, it was particularly quiet and dark.

Within half an hour they reached Gugeri Street.

Gugeri Street was situated in a part of Broome that Raj seldom visited. The houses were small and untidy, the lawns unclipped and overgrown with bushes, and beer bottles were strewn on the footpath and the front yards. A three-legged dog chased a bedraggled grey cat that scurried past in front of their bikes like a cloud of evil.

"To have a cat run across your path is a bad omen in India," Raj thought.

Finding house number 32 was not difficult. As the young couple biked past, they found that Nick's house was a cottage with an overgrown front lawn. There was light coming from the house, and Raj noticed that the single-car carport was empty. On either side of the path to the house, there were thick bushes.

"Keep riding," Raj whispered to his reluctant companion. "After a kilometre or two, turn back. I should be finished by then."

Raj leaned his bike against the fence in a dark spot a few houses away and walked towards the house, keeping to the shadows all the time. From outside the fence, he could make out the silhouette of a thin man within the building. On walking up the driveway to the carport, the young doctor noticed beer bottles and syringes lying scattered among the unkempt bushes on either side of his path. It seemed highly likely that this was the house of a junkie.

When Raj's eyes got used to the darkness, he started rummaging through the shelves at the far end of the carport, looking for an incriminating piece of garden hose. About ten minutes had gone by when he was alerted to the sounds of a car braking outside the house. The headlamps turned towards the house, and within no time the young sleuth was behind the bushes next to the carport. The car drove up the driveway into the carport and stopped with a jerk.

At first, because of the darkness, Raj could barely make out a slender man of about six foot emerging from the car and walking towards the house, but as he neared the house, his features became more visible, and the Indian doctor was surprised when he recognised Frank Witherspoon, the autopsy technician. Frank moved as though with purpose towards the house and started banging on the door.

"Open up!" he shouted.

"Whattya want?" The response from inside the house was quite audible to Raj and clearly indicated that Frank was not welcome.

"I want to talk to you!" Frank shouted.

"You can talk from outside!" the man yelled back.

Frank responded with a kick to the door, a kick so powerful that the door flew open with the cracking sound of a lock breaking, and the autopsy technician entered the house cursing and swearing loudly. As the door opened, the light from the house fell on the car, and Raj recognised the blue sedan advertised on the hospital noticeboard. The young sleuth quickly moved to the window and peeped between the blinds.

Mr. Witherspoon stood facing a dishevelled, bearded youth of around eighteen. Raj's heart missed a beat as he saw the knife in the young man's hand.

"If you take one more step, I will kill you." The man's threat was almost inaudible and slurred but was so menacing that the older man stopped right in his tracks.

"Give me my money," the autopsy technician said in an even, composed tone.

"You can take my car, and anyway, you use it as though it's yours."

"I don't want your filthy car. One of these days I'll run over somebody with your car, and the police will come and get you. An Indian doctor barely escaped once, but next time I'll see him in hell."

"I've a buyer. I got a call yesterday."

"You'll be lucky if you get two hundred for that bomb. That won't be a tenth of what you owe me," Frank sneered. "You gimme two grand today, or you'll pay another way for those drugs."

Raj realised, from his spot in the bushes, that he was witnessing a drug deal going wrong.

The younger man responded by walking to the study table nearby and taking out some banknotes. He turned and handed them to Frank, but Frank could see that they were nowhere near two grand. Nick then made a terrible mistake. He left the knife on the table, and no sooner had Frank's left hand received the money than his right hand smashed into the younger man's face. Nick fell backwards, his head hitting the wall. Raj did not wait anymore. Within seconds he was inside the house.

"Leave him alone!" Raj's command sounded like a knife slicing the air.

"Fuck, damn you!" the drug dealer shouted, thoroughly surprised at this unexpected interference, and when he saw his despised coworker, he took a step towards Raj. The young doctor did not hesitate for the counterattack, and before Frank could comprehend what was happening, Raj had stepped forward and chopped at his chin with the base of his right palm. The drug dealer lost his balance. Raj's left hand grabbed the technician's hair and yanked him down, while his right hand came crashing behind his head. Frank collapsed in a heap. The doctor then moved quickly towards Nick. His eyes were open, and he smiled at Raj.

"Tie him up," Raj ordered Nick.

The junkie slowly got up and rolled the drug dealer onto his belly; he then tied his hands behind his back with a bed sheet.

"Step aside," the doctor ordered Nick, who obeyed him like a little boy and moved to a corner. Raj then crouched next to the fallen man and took his pulse. It was normal.

"Please sit down," Raj ordered Nick. "If you try to stand or make any move, I'll have to tie you up." Nick took that threat very seriously, for he was witness to what had happened to his tormentor. He pulled a chair out and sat on it, his chin resting in his cupped hands.

Raj then moved to a corner of the room and dialled triple zero, never taking his eye off the two men.

"Do you want police, ambulance, or fire service?"

"Police," Raj replied.

The line was quickly transferred.

"What's the problem?" the lady at the other end asked.

"I am calling from Thirty-Two Gugeri Street. There's drug-related violence here."

"Your name, please."

"Dr. Raj Thomas. I'm a doctor at Royal Kimberley Hospital."

"We'll soon be there. Is there a life-threatening condition there?"

"No."

"See you soon."

No sooner had he heard a click at the other end than Raj became aware of soft footsteps near the door.

"Vidya," he called. "Come in."

The young lady stepped into the room cautiously, her face ashen as if she was completely drained off blood.

Raj quickly told her what happened. They waited a couple of minutes before they saw lights flashing at the gate.

Raj briefed the two male police officers on what had happened, although he did not tell them the entire truth. He told them that they were riding down the road when they heard screams from the house and had investigated, resulting in their interference because a man's life was in danger. The officers turned Frank around; he was conscious, but his face was blank, and he did not say anything.

"You have the right to remain silent. Anything you say or do may be used against you in a court of law. You have the right to consult a lawyer," a very authoritative voice told the two men.

Frank and Nick were soon handcuffed.

"I can't take them in one car, because of their hostility to each other," the policeman said, dialling for more officers and another car.

"I've a statement to make," Raj said. He then led one of the police officers and Vidya to the bedroom, closing the door after them, thereby making sure they were out of earshot of the two miscreants. Raj then told the officer in his wife's presence what he heard the autopsy technician tell Nick.

"Frank told Nick that he tried running over me, with Nick's car." He then related to them how he almost got run over by a blue car and his altercations with the autopsy technicians. The officer made sure Raj's statement was recorded in his shoulder microphone and took down the statement in a diary, which Raj signed; Vidya and the officer signed as witnesses.

Soon another police car arrived, and both the men were led away. Nick's blue sedan was driven away by the police, and the house was sealed. Before leaving, the officers asked the doctor couple to visit the police station the next day to make further statements.

Raj and Vidya rode back home together. They did not talk much while they rode. The day's events had tired them, and they both wanted to get home and go to sleep.

CHAPTER 30

THE THIRD POLICE INTERVIEW

"You must be happy," Vidya said to Raj the next morning. She was lying on his arm with her face close to his, and he could feel her warm breath on his neck.

"I'm not happy, but I am definitely happier," Raj corrected his wife using the comparative adjective. "Yeah, I'm a lot more relaxed."

Raj jumped out of the bed, suddenly realising it was already eight in the morning.

"I've got to go to work, and then we'll have to go to the police station for the meeting at ten."

Raphael's office was neat and tidy as usual, and his cool demeanour had a calming effect. This time, though, there was another officer with him. Donald Truman was a narcotics detective; Raphael introduced him to Raj and Vidya, and they shook hands.

"May I turn the voice recorder on?" Raphael asked.

"Yeah, of course," Raj answered.

This time Raj told the police officer the entire truth: how his pursuit of the blue car that had run him off the road had taken him to Nick's house and the events that happened there. Raphael was already aware of the arrests that had happened the previous night and also Raj's statement that Frank boasted about trying to run him over with Nick's car. The officers listened to Raj very attentively and did not interrupt him until he had finished the entire story.

"We haven't questioned the two fellows. Your statement is slightly different from what you told the officers last night." As usual, Raphael had done his homework and had perused Raj's statement to the police the night before.

"I did not think that I had the time to tell them everything in the five minutes I had."

The detectives did not make any comment, and they appeared to be happy with Raj's explanation.

"We have to give them access to their lawyers. We've given them a day's time to contact their lawyers," Raphael said.

Donald Truman added, "We found some contraband in Nick's house and some more—" The man stopped for a moment, looking at Raphael as though asking for his approval to continue. "Actually a substantial amount in Nick's car," he continued after getting a nod of approval from Raphael to carry on.

"We cannot give you the details, but in addition to the usual narcotics, we also got hold of..." Raphael got up and walked to a cupboard. He opened it and took out something. "These," he added, coming back to his desk and showing the doctor a couple of vials of Valium. Raj was surprised at this revelation. "Although anybody working in the hospital may have access to injectable drugs, we want to pursue this seriously," the detective continued. "A team has gone to search Frank's house."

The officer took a break from the conversation and looked at the Indian couple.

"Thanks very much," Vidya said, looking at Raj and trying to read his thoughts before continuing. "Well, we have something to add, something we hadn't told you, because we didn't think it was important." Vidya then told the detectives about the vials of

Valium and insulin she had found in Raj's car the day she returned from Adelaide and found him unconscious in his unit.

"I'm sorry I didn't tell you this. I thought Raj was using Valium because he couldn't go to sleep because of his stomach pain. But he told me he never used it."

"Okay, I understand—but insulin, why should he need that?" the inspector asked, looking at Vidya.

"Well, let me explain," Raj said. "Vidya thought I had pancreatic cancer, which can result in diabetes. She thought I was taking insulin for diabetes and Valium because I could not go to sleep."

"Do you have the vials with you?" Raphael asked.

"Not here, but we have them back at the house. We'll get them for you."

"Anything more to tell us?" Raphael asked. "Anything, even though you may feel it is not important."

"No, no, sir," Raj replied.

The officer then looked at Vidya.

"No, that's all," she said.

"Well, please bring the vials as soon as possible. We will have to try to match the dates on them." The police officers got up, and both of them shook hands with the two doctors.

Raj and Vidya drove back to the hospital. Raj went to finish the rest of the day's work, while his wife drove home.

CHAPTER 31

LUCY MCMILLAN

Dr. Stich was away the rest of the week. Sarah told Raj that he had gone to Ethiopia for a conference on tropical diseases.

The local newspaper reported the arrest on the front page: "Indian doctors nab alleged narcotics trafficker." Journalists tried contacting Raj and Vidya, but they declined to talk to them. Coworkers tried to bring up the subject in the tearoom and in the corridor, but Raj just smiled and said, "Sorry, no comment." Meanwhile, Raphael called Raj and told him that Frank was not co-operating. Nick had meanwhile corroborated Raj's statement that Frank had tried to run over Raj with Nick's car.

Jack Heath, the other autopsy technician, had gone on stress leave after his mate's arrest, and the pathology department now had two male nurses who had been transferred to fill the roles. Though they were friends through thick and thin, there was no convincing evidence that Jack was party to, or even had any inkling about, Frank's nefarious activities. Jack was shocked and let down by the revelation about his colleague of many years.

The other thing of importance that happened that week was the autopsy of Lucy McMillan. It was about four on Friday afternoon that Raj got the call from the autopsy room advising him of the postmortem.

Lucy McMillan was obese at 150 kilograms. They found it difficult to weigh her and talked about bringing in a crane to move her. Raj and John helped to move her to the autopsy desk, which she filled completely with her fat-filled skin folds flowing over its edges.

The radiology showed a mass in the abdomen surrounding the aorta—the main artery carrying blood from the heart. She was breathless when admitted, but her death was sudden and unexpected. A needle core biopsy done three days prior to her death showed only normal fat tissue. The treating doctor did not have difficulty in convincing the relatives of the need for an autopsy.

"The biopsy obviously missed the lesion. They have yet not invented anything long enough to reach into the retroperitoneum of such overweight people," Dr. Largebone said without looking up from the dissection.

The autopsy was difficult due to the sheer size of the patient and the amount of fat they had to cut through. The pathologists opened the abdominal cavity and removed the intestines in one block. There was a lot of fat in the omentum—the curtain that covers most of the intestine. The uterus and ovaries were normal.

"The retroperitoneum looks normal," Raj said.

"Yes," John agreed. "There is a lot of fat. The dissection has to be careful."

The fat surrounding the aorta appeared normal.

For the first time, Raj found the English pathologist struggling with an autopsy. After taking out the intestines, Dr. Largebone removed the aorta, the inferior vena cava, both kidneys, and the uterus and ovaries. He was sweating when he cut out the entire pad of fat from the retroperitoneum, and for the first time, Raj heard John swear.

"We'll do the microscopy—I'm sure this is a liposarcoma," the English doctor said.

Though liposarcoma, or cancer of the fat tissue, could look like normal fat, in liposarcoma the tumour is usually massive, making it very obvious to the naked eye that the tissue is abnormal.

"I do not think there is any liposarcoma." This was the first time Raj contradicted his much-read colleague.

"Well, let us see," the English pathologist said. Though John had regained his composure, his usual confidence appeared to have deserted him this time. He selected the bits of tissue to be put in formalin jars for microscopy and suddenly left the autopsy lab without saying another word.

Usually John dictated the autopsy notes and sewed up the body himself, since the autopsy technicians cared less, but today he was gone before he finished his usual chores, leaving them for Raj to complete. He did not mind, but he did think it was unusual that Dr. Largebone did not want to dictate the notes and take the case for himself. Raj dutifully dictated the autopsy notes and helped the substitute technicians sew and clean the body, following which he had a shower in the bathroom adjacent to the autopsy room. When he walked back to his car, he was slightly unsettled; Lucy's name reminded him of something. "Did it sound familiar? Maybe I saw one of her biopsies," he wondered when he drove back to his house.

"You do not look okay," Vidya stated.

"No, I do not," Raj agreed.

Raj was in no mood for talk or for dinner, and he fell asleep, much to Vidya's annoyance.

That night Raj dreamt he was performing an autopsy. There was another pathologist assisting him, but as he was bent over the body, Raj could not see the other pathologist's face. Suddenly there were footsteps, and when he looked up, he saw Dr. Stich approaching. As the elderly pathologist came closer, his face slowly changed into that of a hyena. Blood dripped from his open mouth and drooled down his whiskers.

Raj screamed and turned to run the other way, but Frank and Jack, the autopsy technicians, were slowly approaching from the other side. As they came closer, their faces also transformed into those of hyenas. The pathologist, who was bent over the body, straightened, but when Raj looked at him, he saw that he lacked a head; where his head should have been was a dark void. The young doctor yelled and started running, with the beasts chasing him, until he fell into a ravine, a ravine full of bodies, all of them naked and disembowelled. Lucy, the obese lady he had just autopsied, slowly sat up from among the dead bodies, her entrails hanging out through a big opening in her abdomen. She raised her hand pleadingly. Raj looked at himself and, to his horror, saw that his own entrails were hanging out.

Raj woke up with a scream.

"What happened? Why are you sweating?" Vidya was concerned, but Raj did not reply and drifted back to sleep.

The next day Raj woke up with a headache. As it was a Saturday, the young doctors decided to go for a walk, and that day they strolled to the hospital and walked past the lightning-struck eucalyptus tree.

"Shall we go and inspect?" Raj suggested to his wife, and she readily agreed.

They left the path and walked to the ancient tree, but only when they got close did they realise how big the monster was. The big mouth-like opening on the trunk was about twenty feet above them.

"Let's go around and have a look," Raj said.

As the couple walked around the tree, dodging the small bushes that surrounded it, they noticed a gorge on the tree trunk leading from the bottom to the mouth-like opening at the top. There were a few small branches around the mouth like bristles of hair on a bald head, but in addition, there were two big horizontal branches that looked like the arms of an ogre below a head without a neck.

Without saying a word, Raj started climbing the tree using nooks in the gorge as footholds.

"What are you doing?" his wife yelled. "Don't you know it is sacred?"

"Well, I'm not destroying it!" the young man shouted back, and he continued to climb till he reached the top, where he slowly eased himself into the hole. The mouth itself was shallow, and Raj could comfortably stand in the hollow of the tree. As he moved around, he sensed that the floor was different and harder in one area. As he bent and felt around, Raj understood that he was standing on an inverted wok-like metal plate about two feet wide. The young man lifted the plate, and he saw it was covering a hole in the floor of the mouth, big enough to admit a twelve-year-old child. Raj put his hand through the hole and felt around. It appeared that the hole expanded into another compartment below.

Suddenly Raj stopped and sniffed the air. There was a faint but definite smell, a smell he was familiar with, and it appeared to be coming from the hole in the floor of the mouth.

"Does it smell like disinfectant?" Raj asked himself. "Or like Dr. Stich's insect spray?"

Raj did not stay there for long.

"We will have to come back and find out what is there in the compartment below," Raj told Vidya after explaining to her what he had found.

CHAPTER 32

THE SHOWDOWN

Monday came, and so did Dr. Stich after his African journey. He spent most of the morning on the phone.

"There are some QAP slides," Sarah said with a smile.

QAP, or quality assurance program, slides were sent out by the Royal College of Pathologists once every other month. Pathologists were required to report on them and send the reports back to the college. The college would then evaluate the slides as a quality assurance service for their fellows. As usual, Dr. Stich contacted his colleagues from all over Australia to get the answers to the QAP slides. It was about two o'clock in the afternoon when Raj took his tray of slides to the elderly pathologist to review. Dr. Stich was standing near his office desk deep in thought.

"Good afternoon, Dr. Stich," the young doctor said.

Dr. Stich nodded his head and then pointed to the tray of slides Raj was taking to him and said dryly, "Why did you put your pubic hair on this?"

As Raj looked at the tray, he saw a single hair on the slide tray, which probably had fallen from his hand. Without uttering a word, the young pathologist quietly put the tray on the desk.

The Indian doctor's right fist caught Dr. Stich on his chin, and the old bastard sank to the floor, as a piece of pudding would plop if dropped from a height. Blood trickled from his nose.

"Well, I've packed my bags for the flight back to India," Raj said in an even tone. "If you want to go to the police, please go ahead. But in that case, you would be known as the first and only consultant in Australia who got beaten up by his registrar. And any sane person would agree with me that I had the right to beat you up and you deserved a hiding."

Dr. Stich sat gazing at the floor from where he sat like a defeated man. Without saying another word, Raj left the slides on the desk and walked out. Sarah had a shocked expression on her face, but she continued typing as though nothing had happened.

It was not easy explaining everything to Vidya that afternoon, but Raj tried to do so. Vidya listened in disbelief and indignation, and when her husband had finished narrating the incident, she quietly told him to resign and leave with her for Adelaide. This time Raj knew that his time was up and he had to leave, for he had no counter argument.

The next morning Raj came to his office with his resignation letter in his pocket and his mind made up to personally hand over the letter to his boss. Dr. Stich was not in his office, so the pathologist handed over the resignation letter to Sarah.

"Please give this to Dr. Stich."

"What's this?"

"Well, after what happened yesterday, there's no point in my continuing here anymore. I'm leaving for India. I've two weeks of annual leave, which I'll utilise as my notice for resigning."

"Dr. Stich's not in. He rang to say he's not well," Sarah said. "No, it's not anything related to what happened yesterday," she explained, seeing Raj's quizzical face. "He said he had high fever and a stomach upset. He's coming to the hospital in the afternoon to see the physician."

Raj did not waste any more time there. "Please say bye to John for me," he asked of Sarah, before heading home to Vidya.

CHAPTER 33

THE TREE

The next three days the young couple were busy planning and making arrangements to leave Broome. They put an ad in the community paper for a lawn sale and visited the few friends that they had made in the short period. Joseph Varghese, their elderly friend, was quite upset when he heard they were leaving.

They were having dinner at Joseph's place that Thursday when Raj received a text message from an old friend he had not seen for a while.

"Please come to the hospital café tonight, if possible," the message read.

They went back home after dinner that night at around nine.

While they were driving home, Raj mentioned to his wife that he had to visit the hospital that night.

"Why? What makes you go there tonight?"

"Well, I need to say good-bye to an old friend."

Vidya looked at her husband for a moment but made no further enquiries.

When Raj came back home after the meeting at around eleven that night, his wife was fast asleep.

The next morning, she also did not ask Raj whom he had visited the previous night.

"Before we go, I have one more thing to do," Raj said that morning.

"What is it?"

"I want to know what is there in the lower compartment of the tree. I am going to hack my way into the lower compartment."

"You could be arrested for that."

Raj did not reply to this. Though the rest of that Friday was spent packing, the young man found time to buy a sharp handsaw.

Sarah rang that afternoon and told Raj that Dr. Stich had been admitted to the hospital.

"I've been to see him. He has a high fever and rashes all over," Sarah said without much emotion.

Sarah also told Raj that Dr. Largebone was managing the department in Dr. Stich's absence and that he was doing that job very well indeed. John seemed concerned about Dr. Stich's health, and the English doctor knew nothing of the altercation between Raj and Dr. Stich. As Raj had expected, Dr. Stich had kept mum about it.

There were two more days until their flight to Adelaide.

That evening the young couple set off to carry out their plans to explore the lightning-struck gum tree. It was around seven in the evening when they drove to the hospital car park in dark outfits. They took with them a large backpack containing the handsaw and an electric lantern.

Even though the monsoon clouds and the new moon ensured that the night was very dark, the young detectives could make out the monstrous tree silhouetted against a dark sky lit occasionally by lightning streaks. Both of them did not dare to talk, as the rumble of distant thunder lent ominous background music to their nocturnal adventure. The young Indian pathologist almost felt lightning pass through his body as they neared the tree.

They had no difficulty in finding the gorge on the tree trunk.

"Maybe you should climb first," Raj requested his wife, as he wanted to stay on guard to ensure they were not discovered. Once Vidya had reached the top, Raj climbed after her, and when they were both inside the hollow of the tree trunk, he switched the lantern on. The faint glow was enough for them to work, and without a word, the young man started sawing the mouth of the hole on the floor of the hollow in the tree trunk. He wanted to make the hole larger so that he could explore the space in the tree trunk below. The work was slow and painful, and they took turns at sawing. After almost two hours, they had cut a semilunar piece of wood from the mouth of the hole, which was wide enough to admit both of them, but by this time the lantern had run out of power.

"We will have to go back," Raj said in a disappointed voice.

Vidya dipped her hand into her pocket and brought out a candle and a match.

"You think of everything, don't you?" The young man was surprised and at the same time very appreciative of his wife.

The two detectives lowered themselves through the hole, and though it was pitch dark inside the tree trunk, once they were inside, they found they could stand straight. Raj struck the match and lit the candle.

"Oh my God!" Vidya exclaimed when she surveyed the inside of the tree trunk.

The space was as big as a small room, and the young couple were amazed at what they saw when they looked around. There were multiple shelves built into the tree trunk, and arranged neatly on these shelves were rows and rows of jars of all sizes.

Raj brought the candle close to one of the bottles, and it was now his turn to gasp. The bottle had neat typewritten labels. "Paul Winter—Melioidosis—Kidney." The next jar was much larger and contained a large piece of Paul Winter's liver. Altogether there were five jars belonging to Paul Winter: kidney, liver, brain, spleen, and testis.

"My God," the young man whispered. "This is one of my early autopsies. This is the American soldier who died of melioidosis. Remember, I told you about him." The young man then shifted his gaze to the next set of jars. "Sonia Gairdner—Strongyloidiasis—Small Intestine."

Altogether there were about thirty-five small and large jars, including Elizabeth Peacock's oesophagus and kidney.

"Most of these are my autopsies," Raj whispered.

"Yours?"

"Yes, I did many of these with John."

Raj and Vidya examined each shelf until they reached the last set of shelves. These were stacked with much smaller vials, and Raj took one of them and examined it under candlelight.

"Insulin," Raj read out the label. Raj took the next vial. "Adrenalin," its label read. There were in addition vials of diazepam.

"Who would bring these here? And store them so neatly?" Vidya muttered. She took the candle from Raj and went back to the first shelf, turning her back on Raj. Her eyes fell on a neatly folded paper on the shelf, which she started to unfold.

There was an empty space next to the last set of shelves, and Raj took a step back to lean on the tree trunk, and *whoom*, he disappeared with a scream, "Eeeyoooh!"

Startled, Vidya turned around and was horrified to see that her husband was no longer in the hollow of the tree trunk.

CHAPTER 34

THE THICKENING PLOT

"Raaaaaaaaaaaaaaaj!" she screamed three times. Getting no response, she clutched the candle and the folded piece of paper and gingerly stepped to where Raj had been standing. Without warning, the floor beneath her feet gave way, and she too fell feet first.

"Eeeyoooh!" Vidya screamed, echoing her husband as she felt herself sliding downwards. She landed with a thud partly on mud and partly on her husband.

Raj groaned loudly and, after gingerly moving his wife from on top of him, slowly sat up. Feeling around in the pitch darkness, he grabbed his wife's arm and pulled her up so that she sat next to him.

"Oh my God!" she groaned.

Raj slowly stood up and took a few steps.

"Where are you going?" asked Vidya.

"Just checking to see if I have any broken bones. See if you can stand." As soon as he said this, Raj walked back and, in the utter darkness, tripped on his wife and almost fell over.

"Let me see if we can find the candle," Vidya muttered. She had let go of the candle and the folded paper when she fell. They both got on their knees and groped in the sand. The tree trunk was much narrower here than the space above.

After about ten minutes, the young man got the candle stump back, and since his wife had another match in her pocket, they lit the candle. They were in the bottom of the tree trunk, and as they looked around, they saw narrow winding steps carved into the wall of the trunk reaching to the trap door on the ceiling or floor of the space where they had entered first. Steel handles were screwed into the tree trunk next to the winding steps for support. From where they stood, the trunk opened into a closed concrete-lined canal about four feet in height.

The folded piece of paper that Vidya had found had fallen on the floor, a little distance away from them, and she stooped to pick it up.

The young couple could hear the heavy rolling of thunder above.

"Please hold the candle for me," Vidya instructed her husband. She knelt on the ground and unfolded the piece of paper while her husband stooped over her. They found that it was a neatly drawn map of what appeared to be a main road with several intersections with narrow roads. Next to one of the narrow roads was the picture of a tree.

"See this? I am sure it is this tree," Raj muttered, "and this is the map of the storm-water drainage."

"Look, there's an *X* marked here." Vidya pointed to the *X* on the map marked next to one of the intersections.

"It is near the twelfth intersection from ours," Raj said after having counted the number of intersections. "C'mon, we have to go!"

"Go where?" Vidya didn't appear to understand.

"Go to the X. Please hand me the candle, and follow me."

Without waiting for an answer, the young man took the candle from his wife and crept into the storm-water drain on all fours.

Vidya was not prepared for this, but there was nothing else she could do but follow her husband, and she crept into the drain after him.

After about fifteen metres from where they had started, the young adventurers found that their knees were very sore, but they kept going. Though they were deep in the drain, they could hear the thunder rolling like the muffled shots from a machine gun several miles away. They had crawled about twenty metres when Raj found the tunnel opening suddenly into a much more voluminous cavernous space, also lined with concrete.

"I think I've reached the main canal!" the young man shouted to his wife.

Raj sat on the ledge with his feet hanging down into the main canal, and in the dim light of the candle, he calculated the entrance to the main canal to be around seven feet deep. He handed the candle to his wife and, after slowly lowering himself into the main canal, reached for the candle that Vidya gave to him before following her husband down into the main canal.

The young couple found that they could now stand straight; in fact, the ceiling was almost two metres high here.

"Hey, my feet are wet," Vidya cried. Without warning, water had started gushing down the storm-water drain, and in a few seconds, it had risen well above their ankles.

"C'mon, quick!" Raj started striding in the direction of the X marked on the map, and his wife struggled to keep up. The water level rose quickly, and in no time they were knee-deep in water. They both took off their shoes and walked about another one hundred metres when they saw water pouring down like waterfalls from the smaller drains on either side.

"The first intersection!" Raj yelled to his wife. "Only eleven more!"

They were walking against the flow of water, which made their progress slow, but they kept on walking. Each intersection seemed to be about thirty metres apart, and by the time they reached the eighth, they were waist-deep in water.

"I can't walk any further," Vidya's voice was almost pleading.

"Take off your pants." Raj took his pants off and put them on his neck like a shawl. "There is less resistance without clothes."

Vidya took off her pants too. It must have taken them half an hour to reach the tenth intersection, and now the water was up to her breasts, and Raj found it difficult to hold the candle above the water level.

"They will never find our bodies," Vidya muttered dejectedly. She was certain their lives were going to end in a watery grave in remote northern Australia.

As if in answer to her desperate thought, Raj took hold of his wife's hand. He realised that for his wife, the water was up to her breasts.

"Only sixty meters, and you are not going to die," he told her. With one hand he held his wife's hand, while his other hand held the now low-burning candle aloft. The young couple kept on moving, their backs rubbing against the wall of the storm-water drain.

It seemed like an eternity when they reached the twelfth intersection. Water was gushing out of the connecting drain above on the side.

"Climb on my shoulder, and get into the side drain," Raj ordered his wife, moving to one side of the torrent.

With water gushing out of the side drain above them, Vidya found it impossible to get into it even though it was not full. She tried several times to get a hold of something in the rushing water but could not. Suddenly she slipped and fell off her husband's shoulder and started floating away. Raj quickly grabbed her hair and pulled her to him, and she clung to him for dear life, consternation gripping her face. Raj understood the grave danger they were in; there was no way they could swim against the current, and if they decided to float along with it, they were sure to get sucked into the drain, where its height was low, and drown. Water was now up to his neck, and they both knew that it was too deep for Vidya to stand. And then the candle went out, and it was pitch dark.

Raj could hear his wife's sobbing. "I am sorry, darling," he said.

Then the young man realised that the sound of water falling from the drain above had reduced in intensity. The water level was not rising anymore; in fact, it had fallen to Raj's shoulder.

"O God, help us," the young doctor prayed. "Baby," he said, "I think you can stand now." Vidya gingerly put her foot down and stood up; the water was up to her neck, but she could stand.

They stood there without moving, hugging each other, and it was about half an hour later, when the water was down to their waist, that Raj slowly released his grip on his wife. He inhaled deeply, thanking his Maker, and then kissing his wife fondly on the lips.

"We will have to get out before the next rain," he said. The water falling from the drain above had now reduced to a trickle.

Suddenly Raj felt something like a handle on the side of the drain. He moved closer, and his body brushed against another handle.

"There are handles screwed onto the wall," he said. He guided Vidya's hand to one of them, and she found another one a bit higher.

"I can feel them." She pulled herself up and climbed the wall slowly, feeling with her feet and hands for the handles screwed on the wall of the drain. The young man followed his wife, and soon they were both crouching in the smaller drain.

"There should be a manhole here," the young doctor muttered while crawling after his wife in the darkness, all the time feeling with his hand on the roof of the drain. They would have crawled some ten metres when the young man felt an edge to the roof. He pushed up, and the concrete slab covering the manhole lifted, allowing faint light from an adjacent street lamp to creep in. It was not difficult to move the concrete slab to one side, and Raj could now stand up, his head and shoulders now outside the drain.

Raj ducked back into the drain, and Vidya, who was ahead, came back and poked her head out. Raj lifted her, and she climbed out of the drain, followed by her husband. The young man dragged the slab back on to the manhole and then turned and gave his wife a long kiss on her lips.

They were both dripping wet, and they put their trousers back on after wringing them to get rid of some of the water. The place seemed familiar to them.

"Hey, I recognise this place," the young man said. They were standing in front of John's unit.

"C'mon!" urged Raj, who briskly walked towards the English doctor's house. The lights in the unit were out, and the front door was locked.

"We have to get in," the young doctor said.

"Call the police."

The young man did not wait to respond to his wife's suggestion but took a few steps back before rushing at the door and hitting it with all his strength with his shoulder. The door flew open as if it were made of cardboard. He turned the lights on and then went straight for the shelf above John's study table from where he took out a large folder. He put the folder on the table and turned the first page.

"Paul Winter," he read. "I told you about the American soldier who died of melioidosis," the young man muttered without taking his eyes off the folder.

The autopsy notes were arranged in chronological order. Before each patient's notes, the clinical history garnered from the patients' charts and pathology investigations from the computer files were arranged neatly.

Paul Winter, Sonia Gairdner, Elizabeth Peacock, Lucy McMillan.

"I now remember why I recognised Lucy McMillan's name when I did her autopsy. I had seen her clinical notes before she died."

"Where did you see her notes?"

"Well, I saw the notes in this folder when we came to deliver the curry after John helped us install the security cameras."

Raj's head spun when he leafed through the pages. He read, "Raj Kurian Thomas, Clinical history: Jaundice of waxing and waning nature." The next ten pages were a detailed account of Raj's illness and clinical investigations. For obvious reasons, there were no autopsy notes. But there were some notes and Raj's blood picture findings of ovalocytosis.

He turned the pages and reached the last patient in the folder.

"Dr. Freiderich S. Stich. Clinical history: Febrile illness with rashes following a journey to Africa."

The young doctor continued reading, with his wife leaning over him and also straining to read. "A sixty-two-year-old, semi-retired pathologist presented at Royal Kimberley Hospital with a seven-day history of fever, diarrhoea, vomiting, and rash. Three days before the onset of symptoms, he had returned from a week's conference in Ethiopia."

Raj suddenly stood up.

"We don't have time to lose. Follow me." So saying, Raj quickly got up and, grabbing the file, looked around.

"What are you looking for?" Vidya asked him.

"I want to hide this, in case John comes back and destroys it." He pulled a dining chair into the far end of the corridor. Standing on the chair, he pushed the ceiling manhole cover to one side and deposited the file in the ceiling space, after which he pulled the manhole cover back in place.

He then put the dining chair back in its place at the table, and they both walked briskly out of the house. Vidya did not quite understand what her husband was trying to do, but she followed him.

The way to the hospital seemed longer than usual, and in between breaths, the young lady quizzically looked at her husband.

"Why is your medical history in his autopsy register?"

"The only reason I can think of"—Raj paused for breath, but when he resumed, Vidya got the shock of her life—"is that he was sure he would be doing an autopsy on me."

"You mean..."

"Yeah, I mean he was the one who tried to murder me—to gas me."

"And Dr. Stich?"

"The next victim. Although he is an arsehole, I do not want him to be killed by a madman."

They were now inside the hospital, and the couple ran up the flight of stairs to the first floor, where the ICU was situated. Without a swipe card, they could not enter the intensive-care unit. Raj picked up the phone hanging on the wall.

"ICU visiting time is from eight a.m. to ten a.m. and from four p.m. to eight p.m.," the automatic message announced from the other end of the phone. Just then the door opened, and a nurse walked out. Before the door shut, Raj was inside the ICU, while his wife was left waiting outside.

There was nobody at the nursing station, and the young pathologist walked straight into one of the cubicles, where a nurse was attending to a patient.

"Who are you, and what do you want? How did you get in?" The nurse obviously did not like the dishevelled intruder who had walked in.

"I am Dr. Raj Thomas, pathology registrar, and I am looking for my boss, Dr. Stich."

"Dr. Stich was transferred to Perth, and he left five minutes ago. Now you have to leave, or I will have to call Security."

"I will leave as soon as you tell me how Dr. Stich left the hospital."

"He was taken to the airport by ambulance, and from there he will leave by plane. Dr. Largebone is going with him."

"Thank you." Without waiting for a reply, Raj turned and in no time was out of the intensive-care building. He grabbed his wife's hand and pulled her along.

"C'mon, we may still save him!"

CHAPTER 35

A RACE AGAINST TIME

Raj led the way to their car, and while running, he told his wife about Dr. Stich's transfer to Perth accompanied by Dr. John Largebone.

"We should be able to catch them at the airport."

Within two minutes, they had got into the car, and the jalopy screeched out of the hospital car park onto Robinson Road. Soon they turned right into Anne Street, but when they attempted to turn right at Herbert Street, there was to their chagrin a "Detour" sign. There was an accident on Herbert Street, and a police car had blocked it off.

"Oh fuck!" Raj was not a person who normally swore, but today he was at the end of his tether, and civility was the least of his concerns. They continued on Anne Street another five hundred metres and a minute later turned right into Tang Street and then left into Kerr Street, but no sooner had they turned into the next street, which was called Lyon Street, than they saw an army of people about a hundred metres away and walking towards them, filling the road. Raj brought their car to a sudden stop. A ute drove past them and stopped a few metres in front of them, and two women jumped out, picking up witches hats from the tray of the ute and placing them on the road in front of them.

Soon Raj's car was swamped by a crowd leaving an Aussie Rules football match, like an island surrounded by a sea of humanity. The doctors got out of their car, and the young man caught hold of his wife's hand and pulled her through the crowd, past the gates of the oval and into the grounds. Most of the people had left, and the oval was empty, with only the cameramen and some ground crew, who were packing up.

"C'mon, the airport is across the oval!" the young man shouted to his wife. Without waiting for an answer, he started running across the oval with her just behind him. They were both exhausted by the time they reached the other side and soon joined the dwindling crowd leaving the oval from the opposite side.

The airport was only a couple of hundred metres from this side of the oval, and soon they were at the security screen within the airport. The officer, a young lanky African man, stared at the dishevelled couple as though he were watching the climax of a horror movie.

"Where are you heading?"

"Flying doctor flight to Perth, carrying one of our patients," Raj explained slowly and carefully.

"Flying doctor?"

"Yeah."

"We've no flying doctors here, only doctors who walk. Maybe you want the CareFlight?"

"Oh yeah, CareFlight. Where is it?"

"Not here. Go out through the main door and another three hundred metres down the road."

"C'mon," the young doctor said, turning to his wife. Vidya looked as though she would collapse any moment.

The CareFlight building was a small nondescript shack at the end of the road inside the aerodrome complex.

The dishevelled couple entered the building, panting and exhausted. There was a paramedic walking across the hall pushing a medicine trolley. He stopped in his tracks as though he were being visited by the devil himself from the depths of hell.

"Hey, what do you want?"

"CareFlight to Perth..." Raj paused to catch his breath.

"What about it?"

"Has it taken off?"

"It's about to fly any minute. What do you want?"

As they shifted their gaze, the doctor couple caught sight of a small plane sitting on the tarmac. The young doctor grabbed his wife's hand, and they ran out towards it. The paramedic was taken aback for a moment with the sudden gust of action, but he regained his senses and ran after the pair.

There was a flight attendant at the door of the small aircraft talking to the man minding the small staircase. She heard the commotion and screamed when she saw running towards her the bedraggled couple with the paramedic chasing them.

Raj ran up the stairs, and before she realised it, the young man had pushed the flight attendant aside and was inside the aircraft. The pilot, who was checking the instruments, turned around and jumped up. Dr. Stich lay on a bed on the right side of the aircraft, his face ashen and his eyes staring lifelessly at the ceiling. Dr. Largebone was unbuckling his seat belt and getting up.

"You bastard!" he hissed and took one step towards Raj.

Raj's right hand smashed into John's windpipe, and he uttered a groan, his knees folding under him. The spindly man fell headlong onto the floor. Without wasting a moment, the Indian doctor picked up the fallen man by his belt and the back of his collar and threw him head first at the advancing pilot, who fell backwards when the human missile crashed into him.

Just then the flight attendant popped into the plane, followed by Vidya.

"Oh my God!" the flight attendant uttered when she saw the devastation inside. Vidya motioned her to be quiet, and turning towards the door, she crouched and unhooked the staircase and pushed it away with her feet. The young lady then closed the aircraft door after the staircase, with the paramedic halfway up it, had rolled away.

"This man will die if you interfere with me," Raj's words appeared to have an effect, and the pilot, who had pushed Dr. Largebone aside and advanced on Raj, stopped in his tracks.

The small video screen behind the bed showed a slow pulse wave of just thirty beats per minute. Raj felt Dr. Stich's pulse. He could feel a faint throbbing.

"Start resuscitation!" Raj shouted as he moved to the back of the plane and opened the medicine cupboard. It didn't take him long to identify a fifty-millilitre vial of 50 percent glucose, which he grabbed along with a twenty-millilitre syringe.

Vidya was kneeling on the bed and had the base of her hand on Dr. Stich's chest. She pressed his chest and was counting one, two, three...

Raj broke the vial and drew the glucose into the syringe, before disconnecting the intravenous line from the needle on Dr. Stich's arm with deft hands.

"Look out!" Vidya screamed, and Raj turned his head. From the corner of his eye, he saw the flash of a knife. Raj ducked instinctively. The knife came back in a sweeping arc, and this time the young doctor was ready. From a bent position, he went into a crouch and caught the knife handle just below the wrist with his right hand. Raj's left hand grabbed the Englishman's upper arm, twisting it. He threw the man down; the knife flew from John's hand to the floor.

"Give him the glucose!" the young doctor shouted to his wife before turning Dr. Largebone onto his belly and tying his hands behind his back with his own belt. He then put his hands into the English doctor's trouser pockets and fished out two vials of medicine.

"I want all of you to see this." Raj showed the flight staff what he had confiscated from John's pockets and put it on the desk at the head of the patient's bed.

By this time Vidya had finished injecting Dr. Stich with the glucose, watched by the pilot and the flight attendant.

Dr. Stich opened his eyes. "Where am I?" he asked.

"In hell," Raj answered.

There was loud banging on the door.

"I think you can open the door now," the young doctor told the flight attendant, who promptly did just that.

An authoritative male voice shouted, "This is the police! Everyone inside come out with your hands up!"

"Vidya, you go out, just as he asks, with your hands above your head. Explain what is happening, and tell them I cannot leave the patient now, or he might die."

The young lady looked at her husband for a second and slowly walked to the door with her hands up, followed by the flight attendant, also with her hands up.

Vidya stopped at the door and said, "Listen, I want you to hear what I have to say."

The response to this was not irrational, but to the young woman, alien to the ways of the law-enforcement world, it was unexpected. "You are under arrest. You are entitled to have a lawyer, but anything you say may be used against you."

Vidya turned and looked at her husband, searching for his advice.

"Tell them to come inside," he advised her.

Vidya turned towards the policeman and shouted clearly. "We do not have any weapons. We are doctors. We are trying to save a life. If we come out, the man inside may die, and you will be held responsible. If you come inside, we will explain it to you." So saying, she moved to the side and out of view of the policemen outside.

The pilot, who had been a witness to the drama, slowly moved to the door with his hands up. "I'm the pilot of this plane."

"You can lower your hands and come down" was the response from the officer outside.

The pilot got off the plane, and the flight attendant slowly moved to the door.

"I want you to stay here and be our witness." Raj paused for a minute before continuing, "I request you." The flight attendant stopped in her tracks and slowly turned back. She moved to the flight attendant's seat and sat down.

They might have waited around twenty minutes, during which time the young doctors were attending to the patient, who lay there staring at the ceiling. His vital signs were improving. Dr. Largebone occasionally stirred and wiggled but did not make any serious attempt to get up.

After about twenty minutes, they heard footsteps coming up the staircase. A male police officer entered, followed by a female officer. Raj was sitting on the chair next to the patient's seat, and he got up. The officers did not shake hands with them, but the male officer took the seat vacated by the Indian doctor and took out his diary.

"I still have to repeat that you are entitled to a lawyer, and what you say may be taken against you. You should also know that this conversation is being recorded." The officer pointed to his shoulder microphone.

"I understand that," the Indian doctor replied. "I believe that this man," Raj pointed to Dr. Largebone, "tried to murder this man," he said, pointing to Dr. Stich.

"Why do you think so?"

"I can answer that question only if the assailant is removed from the scene," Raj responded.

The male police officer got up and walked to where John was lying and untied him. John turned onto his back and stared at the officer.

"Do you agree with what that man said, or do you deny it?"

"I did not try to kill anybody. This man is interfering with the duty of a doctor, and he is endangering the life of a patient," John said in his usual confident and clipped accent, staring at the policeman, who turned and looked at Raj.

There was another flurry of footsteps up the staircase, and the pilot, followed by a woman of around twenty-five, entered the cabin.

"This is the new doctor who is taking care of the patient," the pilot explained. "We will be flying in ten minutes, if the doctor agrees."

Raj turned to the doctor and introduced himself. "I am Dr. Raj Thomas, pathology registrar, and this is my wife, Dr. Vidya Thomas. Dr. Stich is out of immediate danger. He had an attack of severe hypoglycaemia following an injection of insulin. I have given him a dextrose injection of fifty cc, and he has recovered from his hypoglycaemia. He is suffering from a tropical infection from which I believe he is recovering."

"I'm Dr. Natalie Crocker," the woman said, shaking hands with Raj and then with Vidya. "Is the patient diabetic?" she asked.

"No."

"Why, then, is he on insulin?"

"He was given insulin when it was not required, and I believe it was deliberate." Raj then turned and pointed to the medicine vial he had fished out of Dr. Largebone's pocket. "I have touched it, but please use gloves to hold it. The fingerprints may be important."

Natalie quickly donned a pair of gloves and gingerly took the vials from the desk and read, "Injection insulin."

The police officers turned towards the pilot and the flight attendant, and as if on cue, they said in unison, "We saw this man pulling it out of the doctor's pocket," both pointing to Dr. Largebone.

Raj walked to the medical-waste bin and opened the lid. "The syringe which was used to inject the insulin is here," he said, handing the bin to Natalie, who took the syringe from the bin and handed it and the vials of insulin to the female officer who was standing next to her. The officer took a towel from her pocket and received the articles from Dr. Crocker, after which she wrapped the articles in a towel and deposited them in her pocket.

The attention of the small crowd turned to John. His face appeared drained, and his usual confidence was no longer there.

The lady police officer walked to Dr. Stich's bed. "Sir, how are you?"

"I feel all right. I don't understand what is happening."

Now it was Dr. Crocker's turn to ask a question. "Sir, I am Dr. Natalie Crocker, and I am going to look after you. Please tell me, are you diabetic?" Dr. Stich shook his head. She picked up the patient's notes from the file holder attached to his cot and started skimming them. "There is no mention of diabetes anywhere here, and the treatment schedule does not talk about the management of diabetes," she said after a few minutes.

"I'm taking you into custody," said the male police officer, who helped John to his feet and led him out of the plane. The officer came back in a few minutes.

"I need you both to come with me to the police station," the officer said, shifting his gaze between Raj and his wife.

Dr. Crocker was already checking Dr. Stich's vital signs and taking notes.

The male police officer said, "I think we have to go now. You're both coming with us to the police station." He motioned to Raj and Vidya, and they followed him out of the plane, and the female officer in turn followed them.

The young doctor couple, accompanied by the officers, had a quick meal in the city cafeteria, following which they were taken to their home, where they showered and changed clothes. All this time the officers stayed with them. They then took the doctors to the police station. Raj and Vidya were asked to remain in police custody at the police station that night. They slept in separate cells. It was past midnight when they went to sleep, and it was about ten in the morning when they got up.

The next morning the doctor couple were made to give their statements separately. They finished late in the afternoon, and then Raj and Vidya took the police officers to John's unit, where Raj took out John's folder from the ceiling space and handed it to the police. Then they took the police to the large lightning-struck tree and showed them how they had got inside and the space inside the tree.

CHAPTER 36

THE DEAD SHALL TEACH THE LIVING

Mortui vivos docebunt.
("The dead shall teach the living.")

Raj and Vidya were asked to remain in Broome for a week while the police carried out their investigations.

John Largebone confessed to the murder attempts on Raj and Dr. Stich. He also confessed to killing most of the patients he did autopsies on. He said he did it for the advancement of medicine and to save future lives. His methods of murder made the deaths look natural. Injecting high doses of insulin was one of his favourite methods.

Raj and Vidya were leaving for Adelaide that afternoon, and Vidya had gone to the bedroom to have a nap. Raj put the kettle on and made tea. He brought the cups to the bedroom and sat next to Vidya. She was awake and watching Raj intently.

"What made you look in the tree?"

"It was intuition. I never believed Frank to be intelligent enough to gas me and make it look like suicide. Frank is crafty but not intelligent. The two methods were entirely different."

"What two methods?"

"The two murder attempts. Gassing me was sophisticated, and it was carried out almost to perfection. Edging me to the kerb was crude and fraught with risks. They were completely different in their level of sophistication. The gassing was done by a professional and the other by an amateur."

"So..."

"Yes, so from the time Frank was arrested, I never believed he was responsible for the first attempt. They were done by two different people with a big difference in intelligence."

"I agree with you." Vidya mentally congratulated her husband. "But what made you go after the tree? It was as though you knew something was hidden there."

"I knew the tree was mysterious. Once when I walked past it in the night, I heard the clang of bottles." Raj paused for a moment. "Well, I will tell you. Do you remember my telling you about Maria?"

"You mean the pretty Eritrean girl on whom you had a crush?"

"If you want to put it that way," Raj said, surprised at his wife's comment.

"Well, what about her?"

"She was the one whom I visited that Thursday night after dinner."

Vidya sat up in the bed.

"We met at the hospital café. But she was too scared to talk there, so we drove to her house."

"Was her boyfriend there?"

"Yes, he was. He looked worried as well. We sat in their lounge, and Maria told me about John. John was the person who persuaded Maria to do nursing."

Raj recalled that night in Maria's house.

"Maria left pathology and joined nursing training. She apparently liked it until John started asking her for insulin and other drugs such as diazepam and morphine. John told Maria that the drugs were for personal use and that he was a diabetic and all that."

"Did Maria consent to these demands?" Vidya interrupted him.

"At first she did, but she soon found that there were complaints that vials of medicine were missing from the ward pharmacy. She was very scared that she would be found out and so she stopped doing it. Then she heard that medicine vials were missing from other wards as well. Though she could not prove it, she felt John was probably behind it, and he was stealing the medicine vials during his hours as a doctor in the wards. And then John tried many tricks to entice Maria to help him, like promising to make her his research partner and even threatening to dob her in. John told Maria that he was making a lab in the lightning-struck gum tree."

"And Maria told you all this?"

"Yes, she told me."

"Did she ever have an inkling what he was using the drugs for?"

"No, she did not have an inkling as to what their real purpose was. She thought John was a junkie."

As they started off to the airport later that afternoon, they saw boys playing cricket in the rain.

They drove past the lightning-struck eucalyptus tree. There was a red ribbon cordoning off the tree and a bunch of police officers and reporters in raincoats around the tree.

CRIME SCENE—KEEP OUT, the sign read.

"Please stop for a moment," Raj requested the driver.

The car slowed down and stopped at the edge of the road, and Raj got out into the pouring rain. A streak of sunshine passed through the clouds and lit up Raj's friend Benjora's head. The downpour had caused streams to gush down the mountain—streams of tears of happiness.

"Well done, young fella," he seemed to say.

Raj waved at him and blew a parting kiss to his friend, before he got back in the car.

"Who is that? Whom did you wave to? I didn't see anybody…" Vidya was perplexed.

"An old friend. I shall tell you all about him."

The windscreen wipers worked furiously as the car entered the main road and gathered speed on the way to the airport.

ABOUT THE AUTHOR

 R. M. Kureekattil is a histopathologist and with the help of his friends founded Oz Pathology in Darwin, Australia. He is a fellow of the Royal College of Pathologists of Australasia. In 1999, Kureekattil relocated to Australia from India with his wife, Valentina, who is also a doctor, and their eldest child. The couple had two more children after their move.

Kureekattil drew from his medical experience, particularly in the realm of autopsies, when writing *The Dead Shall Teach the Living*, his first novel.

All the characters, both dead and alive and places in this novel are fictitious.

82420898R00115

Made in the USA
Columbia, SC
16 December 2017